INTERLUDE

SNOW & WINTER COLLECTION: VOLUME ONE

C.S. POE

This is a work of fiction. Names, characters, places, and incidents either are the product of the author's imagination or are used fictitiously, and any resemblance to actual persons, living or dead, business establishments, events, or locales is entirely coincidental.

Interlude
Copyright © 2021 by C.S. Poe

All rights reserved. No part of this book may be reproduced in any form, stored in any retrieval system, or transmitted in any form by any means—electronic, mechanical, photocopy, recording, or otherwise—without prior written permission of the publisher, except as provided by United States of America copyright law. For permission requests and all other inquiries, contact: contact@cspoe.com

Published by Emporium Press
https://www.cspoe.com
contact@cspoe.com

Cover Art by Reese Dante
Cover content is for illustrative purposes only and any person depicted on the cover is a model.

Edited by Tricia Kristufek
Copyedited by Andrea Zimmerman
Proofread by Lyrical Lines

Published 2021.
Printed in the United States of America

Trade Paperback ISBN: 978-1-952133-23-7
Digital eBook ISBN: 978-1-952133-22-0

For the Curious & Mysterious crew.
Thank you for inspiring endless scenarios to get Sebastian
tangled up in.

AUTHOR'S NOTE

In order to best enjoy *Interlude*, please begin with reading the first book in the Snow & Winter series: *The Mystery of Nevermore*.

INTERLUDE

DOPAMINE: TAKE ONLY AS DIRECTED

—

After *The Mystery of Nevermore*
POV: Sebastian Snow

—

"You've got the flu, boss," Max said.

I lay facedown on the bed, my cell on speaker beside my head. "It's not the flu," I weakly protested.

"You have a fever?"

"Uh-huh."

"Chills?"

"I guess."

"Have you barfed?"

"Max—"

"How many times?" he demanded.

"I don't know. Do dry heaves count?"

"I'm calling your dad."

"Do not call my father," I said, doing my best to sound authoritative, but even I could hear that particular note of pathetic in my tone.

To be honest, it probably *was* the flu. It was January—well, it'd be January in about fifteen hours—the season of illness. And don't doctors say stress can weaken your immune system? In the last two weeks, I'd broken up with my boyfriend of four years, found my former boss murdered, gained a stalker, and was shot at. Oh, and had fallen head over heels for an older, newly out-of-the-closet cop who I'd heard very little from since Christmas.

That all might have had something to do with these sniffles.

I shifted in bed and stared at the nightstand. I had a full fucking pharmacy in action: a half-empty bottle of cough syrup, torn-open packages of a few different cold medications I'd been using over the last twenty-four hours, tissues everywhere….

"—run the Emporium myself," Max was saying.

I raised my head from the mattress. "What? No."

"I *can*, Seb."

"I know you can, but you don't have a security code or even any petty cash. Take the day off. Don't worry, I'll pay you."

"Sure, but—"

"Happy New Year," I interrupted.

"Fine. I know when I'm not wanted," Max concluded. "But promise if you get any worse, you'll call your dad or Calvin, yeah? It's hard to pick up a paycheck when you're in the city morgue."

I laid my head down again, frowning at the mere suggestion that Calvin Winter and I were now close enough that he'd be in my Top Three Contacts to whine to when I felt like human excrement. I mean, sure, I had this roller-coaster sensation in my gut whenever I saw him. The indescribable feeling that the personification of home was smiling at me. And he'd spent Christmas with me and Pop too, which I had assumed at the time meant… *something*. Confirmation that he felt about me the way I did him, I guess. Honestly, though, for someone who identified as a guy and had been exclusively into other men his entire life, I really didn't seem to understand jackshit about them.

"Uh-huh," I agreed. "I'm hanging up now."

"Get some rest."

"Thanks." I tapped the End button, turned off the phone screen, and shut my eyes. I welcomed either breathing out of both nostrils or sweet death.

Whichever came first.

I'd probably taken a bit too much cough syrup prior to Max's cross-examination phone call, because when I woke to the sound of my front door opening, I immediately chalked it up to Neil coming home from work. And then the facts, delayed though they were, fanned themselves out for my feverish brain to take in.

I had ended things with Neil. It'd been messy, and he'd moved out just before the holidays. Then, in an attempt to warm Calvin up to the idea of dating—something he had pushed back on during the Nevermore case—I'd given him keys to my place. But he'd not used them once.

"Kiddo?"

That's when the quiet shuffle of steps in the front room finally made sense. It wasn't Neil, who had a quick, almost agitated pace, like he was late and stuck walking behind tourists in Times Square. It wasn't Calvin either, who was heavier on his feet, slow and methodical, but always sure in his destination.

"In here," I called around the marbles in my throat. "But put on a hazmat suit."

Pop opened my bedroom door. "Max called me," he stated.

"That traitor," I mumbled, unmoving.

"He said you were simmering in your own juices."

"I'm a little underdone. Another hour, tops." I pulled the comforter over my head.

Pop sighed, and then the blankets were yanked from the foot of the bed and I was exposed like a newborn baby.

"*Dad*," I whined, adding a few syllables that didn't otherwise exist in polite society.

Pop finished tugging the tucked-in blankets free and dropped the bedding into a pile on the floor. "You smell, Sebastian."

"I definitely do."

"Go take a shower and I'll make your bed."

I sat up, grabbed my glasses, and put them on. "I'm a grown man."

"You're more stubborn than a mule, is what you are." Pop moved to stand in front of me as I planted my feet on the hardwood floor.

"It's a man-cold. I'm being properly dramatic about it."

"Sebastian Andrew Snow."

I winced. "Christ, Dad. Leave Andrew out of this."

Pop pressed his hand to my forehead and frowned. "It's not a man-cold."

"You can diagnose with just the hand-to-forehead

maneuver, huh?"

"Sure," Pop answered, a smile reluctantly tugging at the corner of his mouth. "It's a skill upgrade that comes with being a parent. Now, get in the shower. The hot water will help."

"Fine." I slowly got to my feet, collected clean pajamas from the dresser, and padded into the bathroom. I stripped and stood under scalding-hot water until my toes and asscheeks burned, but with the trade-off being I could breathe, if only momentarily, through both nostrils. After soaping and rinsing, I quickly toweled off as the cold, wintry bite in the air worked its way through the steam and heat of the bathroom. I dressed, but before I stepped out, I caught my reflection in the mirror and grimaced. I looked pale, almost waxy, despite the shower. And I had some serious whisker growth beyond my normal scruff. This was somewhere on the scale between lumberjack and homeless, and no points for guessing which end of the gauge I was flirting with. I started cleaning up with my electric razor, then said fuck it, because who was I looking to impress on New Year's Eve when I was sick and home alone and my not-boyfriend had been radio silent for days?

I walked out of the bathroom and glanced through the open door to our—*my* bedroom.

I wondered how long it'd be before my brain stopped slipping up. Four years was a long time to spend with someone. A lot of memories—good and bad. A lot of experiences—good and bad. A lot of… good and bad, I supposed. Even if I'd fallen out of love with Neil and had only realized it by the time Calvin Winter had been thrust into my shop and my life, seeing my apartment as *mine* and not *ours* was going to take a bit of adjusting to.

Pop had opened the window a few inches, letting brisk air into the room. The cardinals that nested in the tree outside were singing. The bed had been made.

I turned as my dad came out of the kitchen.

He put a teapot and bowl on the table, then sat down. "Come get something to eat, kiddo."

I took a seat, and Pop poured us each a cup of tea. I normally never drank tea, but it'd definitely be easier on my gut than coffee at the moment. I stirred the chicken noodle soup in the bowl—Campbell's, can't go wrong with the classics—then asked, "Do you think I made a mistake?"

Pop took a sip of tea, set his mug down, then tapped his own cheek. "You missed a patch here."

"I did?" I touched my face before saying, "No—I mean—with Neil."

"No." Finality and no room for argument.

I looked down at the soup again, hacking the noodles in half with the side of my spoon. "What about with Calvin?"

"What do you mean?" Pop's tone softened at the mention of Calvin's name.

I shrugged but didn't look up. "I haven't seen him since he spent Christmas with us. He's got my phone number, but has only texted me a few times. He's got a copy of my keys, but hasn't used them. December was a batshit-crazy whirlwind of a month, but he *knows*…. I told him I wanted to date. I mean, is the polite ghosting my answer?" I glanced up over the rims of my glasses.

Pop leaned across the table, put his hand on my wrist, and gave it a firm squeeze. "I think you've been through a lot, Sebastian, and should take it slow for a while."

I let the spoon clatter against the rim of the bowl, took my glasses off, and wiped my face on the sleeve of my shirt.

"Calvin too," Pop continued. "He was shot. And you said he came out to his family—hey, kiddo." Pop stood and moved toward me. He leaned over, wrapped his arms around my shoulders, and pulled me against his chest as I started sobbing like a fucking baby. "I didn't mean to upset you."

"I like him so much," I said, turning to bury my face against Pop. "I never felt this with Marcus or Brian or—even Neil. But every day I don't hear from Calvin… I feel like I'm going to die."

"That's probably the flu."

I choked out a laugh, pulled back, and coughed into the crook of my arm. "You're right. It's the fever talking."

Pop fixed my hair while saying, "I see how he looks at you, Sebastian. He might need some space and some time to figure himself out, but I don't think Calvin's going anywhere."

As he took a step back, I grabbed his hand and asked with a forced lightness in my tone, "Speaking of Calvin looking at me… um… are his eyes green or blue? I know they can't be brown, right? Too light."

"Blue," Pop answered with a nod.

"Blue like what?"

He was thoughtful for a moment, then smiled inwardly. I'd asked this question a lot when I was a kid: Like what? Color meant nothing to me, so when I asked, *blue like what*, I could learn to associate. When I was little, I think that inquiry bothered Pop. It hurt him, as a parent, to see his child struggle to fit into a world that seemed to have no place for him. But eventually, Dad grew to understand why it was an important question for me, how it helped me—at least, how it helped on an intellectual and emotional level, that is.

"Blue like the sky in spring," he answered. "Just after sunrise."

Pop fussed over me for a few more relentless hours before admitting he had to go home to pick up Maggie, his pit bull princess who lunged her fifty pounds of muscle at me on the regular because she *liked me*, for their afternoon volunteer hours at a pittie rescue uptown. Once he was out the door, I migrated to the couch for the afternoon portion of death and decay. I lay sprawled on my side, my toes poking out from underneath a throw blanket, alternating wads of tissue shoved up either nostril when they, at random, became the Niagara Falls of mucus.

And I had to wonder why I was single? Jesus Christ....

At some point, the documentary I'd been half watching on the history of jazz in America had ended and reruns of *Antiques Roadshow* had begun. Neil and I had rarely seen eye-to-eye when it came to sharing the television. I liked black-and-white movies, and my absolute favorites were silent films, starring the likes of Harold Lloyd, Mary Pickford, and my personal favorite, unconventional silver screen heartthrob, Buster Keaton. Neil liked '80s horror and slasher films. I know—the suits and BMW make it *so obvious* what a little bad boy he is. But movies like *The Fly*, *A Nightmare on Elm Street*, *The Evil Dead*—he was crazy for those, so he'd not been too keen on the TV's default channel being PBS. He said I got obsessive about *Antiques Roadshow* the way some people did about *Jeopardy!*, and that arguing with the television over appraisals was weird.

Because Jeff Goldblum being turned into a monstrous fly was fucking *normal*.

My phone buzzed on the coffee table, and I considered ignoring it. It was going to be Max or Pop checking in for the nth time, but I figured they'd keep texting if I didn't respond and then I'd never get to rot in peace. I leaned over, grabbed the cell, and brought it close to my face.

Calvin Winter.

I felt my heart kick into overdrive and immediately lodge itself into my throat.

Happy New Year's Eve, baby. Any plans?

He called me baby. That was good. That was great, in fact. I hadn't realized what a sucker I was for terms of endearment until Calvin had called me sweetheart and baby. And he wouldn't be asking about my plans if he wasn't interested, right? There was no reason for polite small talk in a text that he initiated.

I carefully pecked out a response.

You too. No pln. Udder wether.

I squinted at the screen and swore. "Udder?"

I hastily typed: *Yunder.*

"The fuck is yunder?" But before I'd made a third attempt, the phone started ringing. I nearly dropped it on my face before managing to accept the call. "Uh, hi," I said, my voice croaking a bit.

"You don't sound so good," Calvin answered.

"I am justly kill'd with mine own treachery."

Calvin was quiet for a moment before asking, "Poe?"

"Shakespeare—*Hamlet*," I corrected. "Well, Laertes, to be specific. I think I have the flu. I'm fine, though."

"The flu is serious. You didn't go into work, did you?"

"No, no. I'm home."

"Do you need anything?"

My heart was pounding in my throat again. "Like what?"

"I don't know." Calvin hesitated but then said, "Medicine? Food? I can pick something up and come over."

"Oh. No, don't be silly."

"It's not being silly. I'm concerned."

I quickly turned my head and coughed—the kind where your lungs feel full of broken glass—and then wheezed into the phone, "I'm okay, really. My dad's already been here and thoroughly babied me. And I don't think Max has a New Year's date, because he's texted me, like, five times already….” I cleared my throat before adding, “Besides, you've been shot.”

“I've been shot before,” Calvin replied, quiet and solemn.

“I bet that's not something a lot of people get to say.” Calvin didn't respond, and I scrambled for something semi-intelligent in order to break the silence. “I don't want to get you sick.”

“I know my limits.”

Plucking some lint from the blanket, I murmured, “I appreciate the offer. I've… er, missed you this week.”

“I've missed you too,” Calvin replied, and there was a smile in his words.

“It'd have been nice to ring in the new year together, don't you think?”

Calvin blew out a breath. “I think so.”

“Rain check?”

Instead of answering, Calvin said, “I better let you go.”

“Calvin—”

“Get some rest, sweetheart.”

I screwed my eyes shut and nodded to myself. “Sure. Okay. Bye.” I tapped End, got off the couch, and fetched the NyQuil from the bedroom. After returning to the living room, I pinched my nose, knocked back the disgusting berry-flavored syrup, and waited for the acetaminophen, dextromethorphan, and red #40 to take effect.

The next time I returned to the land of the living, the front room was pitch-black and the television was a blinding beacon that sent spots swimming across my vision. I slowly sat up, wiped my face, and belatedly realized I'd been drooling.

Nice. I'd drugged myself to the gills and nearly drowned

to death.

I found my glasses on the floor and my phone on the coffee table, and squinted as I tapped the home screen. Shit. It was after nine. I'd slept the entire afternoon. I tossed the phone to the cushion beside me and looked around. I wasn't sure what'd woken me so suddenly—

A rap at the door made me jump.

"*Christ.*" I stood, turned on a lamp, stubbed my toe, then limped to the door. I pulled the chain lock free, twisted the deadbolt, and opened it to reveal… an empty landing. I stepped forward and craned my neck to see down the first few steps of the stairwell. "Hello?"

Nothing.

I must have still been stoned from the NyQuil.

I took a step back into the apartment and my bare foot smacked a package on the floor beside the doorframe. I crouched, knees cracking as I collected the item. It was lightweight and flat, like a sheaf of cardboard, and wrapped in Hanukkah paper, which was printed with glittery dreidels.

Across the front, in bold Sharpie, was scrawled:

Bring this to the roof.

-C

C was Calvin, right? I hadn't seen much by way of handwriting samples from him, but I leaned toward this being a man's penmanship, simply based on its appearance. Except, if it was from Calvin, why not wait for me to answer the door and go up to the roof together? Even more important than that—why was he skulking around my rooftop at night in the freezing cold? Had medical leave finally caused him to snap?

Brows furrowed, I glanced to my immediate right at the stairs that led to the fourth floor, which then ultimately led to the roof access. I took another wary step into my apartment, returned to the couch, and picked up my phone. I called Calvin, but after half a dozen rings, his voicemail picked up.

"Detective Calvin Winter. Please leave a message."

I growled, hung up, and grabbed my coat and scarf from the rack beside the open door. I pulled out snow boots from the closet and shoved my bare feet into them. Pocketing my phone, keys, and grabbing the mystery gift, I left the apartment. I trudged to the fourth floor, then rounded the corner and took the final set of stairs to the roof, illuminated only by the glow of an overhead EXIT sign. The metal door screeched obnoxiously as I pushed it opened onto the wintry night. My steps on the pea gravel were momentarily drowned out when I started hacking up a lung, and by the time I'd finished, I was doubled-over, wheezing, and taking in gulps of air when I could catch my breath.

"You okay, baby?"

I turned toward that warm, deep voice and saw Calvin silhouetted by the city's night sky, a gray, blurry halo settled around his head. "S-sure," I managed. "Never been better." I waved the gift while slowly righting myself. "What the heck?"

Calvin stepped out of the saturated light and came toward me. I could make out his arm still in a sling, scarf around his neck, and pea coat thrown over his shoulders. He reached a hand out and touched my face. "You've got a fever."

"Good thing it's below freezing out here." I cleared my throat a few times and then asked in a voice more like my own, "What's going on?"

Calvin smiled, a little sweet and a little shy. "Why don't you open that first?" he said, nodding at the wrapped package.

I gave him a skeptical look.

"The store was selling wrapping paper for 50 percent off. All they had was Hanukkah-themed."

I tried to hum "I Have a Little Dreidel" as I tore the

packaging, but it really just sounded like I was trying to cough up my other lung, so I stopped. I dropped the paper and held up… the spinner board for Twister. "Oh. This is… you shouldn't have."

Calvin chuckled. He wrapped his hand around my nape, and his cold fingers felt so good against my flushed skin. "Come sit down." He led the way toward an open section of rooftop where two lawn chairs were set out, looking north. He dropped into one seat and patted the second.

I perched on the edge of the seat and stated, "I'm not limber enough for naked Twister."

"Why do you assume we'd play naked?"

"I'm not a nine-year-old at a sleepover, and I like how you look without pants."

Another smile flirted across Calvin's face. He dug his phone out of his pocket, saying, "Why don't you give it a spin?"

I'd opened my mouth to protest, to admit to Calvin that the last time I'd been in charge of the spinner was at Craig Gerhart's eighth birthday, and my classmates had howled with laughter when I tried to announce the colors and kept mixing them up, and my dad had to come pick me up early when Craig's mother found me hiding in the linen closet crying. But then I noticed that the same penmanship—Calvin's— had written the color within each circle.

Green. Yellow. Blue. Red.

I bit my lip, flicked the spinner, and announced, "Left foot, blue."

Calvin tapped out a text message, then pointed. "Watch the sky."

"Watch the sky for—" The rest of the question didn't get past my lips as dozens of lights shot up from a street below, surpassed the surrounding rooftops, and swam across the night sky in a silent, coordinated dance. They pulsated from the cores and moved outward in a circular motion, mimicking the explosion of fireworks without actually breaking any city laws by shooting off pyrotechnics. "Oh my God."

"Spin it again."

I glanced at Calvin before hastily flicking the spinner a second time. "Right hand, red."

Calvin sent another text, and then the display altered in design, shifted in light intensity, and reflected what I had to only assume was a bright red. I could feel Calvin watching me, and then his hand returned to my neck. "You all right?"

I nodded and wiped my nose on my coat sleeve. "How're you doing this?"

"Drones. A detective I used to work with in Major Cases is a big techie. He does light shows in place of fireworks in his spare time."

"I bet you're paying a lot of money for this."

Calvin squeezed my nape. "I'm sorry I've been MIA."

"You've had a lot going on."

"Yeah." Calvin nodded. Swallowed. He looked at the sky—the drones were moving in unison like a flock of birds. "I've done a lot of thinking."

I tried to suck in a breath, but my lungs felt like cement balloons. "Okay."

He looked at me again. "Do you like the drones? I thought, maybe a visual representation of the colors at your choosing would make it better. Or different. I don't mean to imply—"

"No, no," I blurted out before hastily wiping my eyes. "I like it. Color association. Being able to decipher different shades of gray. Can I spin it again?"

"Sure."

I flicked it a third time and announced, "Right hand, yellow."

Calvin sent another text and the light show changed once more.

"I'd like to make it official," he said at length, drawing his fingers up the back of my neck and into my hair. "Between us."

"R-really?"

"If I haven't completely thrown away my shot."

I shook my head. "You haven't. I'm still *really* interested. But I understand that being out is still new, so I'm trying not to push you. But I can't go back in the closet either. Not after everything with Neil—"

"Don't ever deny a part of who you are for someone else's comfort," Calvin said firmly. "It's a miserable, shit existence. Understand?"

I softly concurred.

His expression relaxed and he resumed dragging his fingers through my hair. "I have baggage. I think you… know that. But coming out to my family was like the weight that'd been crushing my chest for thirty years was finally lifted. I *do not* regret that. And I know it's important we do that for ourselves, but I did it for you too. Being out is… yeah, it's new and a bit overwhelming, but I'm okay. You're leading the charge, and I *promise*, I'll follow wherever you go."

LUNCH DATE

—

After *The Mystery of Nevermore*
POV: Sebastian Snow

—

"Yes, we have a small collection of black glass buttons," I told the customer on the phone as I stood over the case in question, studying the pieces. "They became in vogue after the passing of Prince Albert. … The masses often followed the trends of—correct. And glass buttons were the more affordable option at the time. Are you looking for a complete set for clothing restoration, or are—? … You're going to do *what* with the buttons?"

A hand snaked around my waist from behind. I jumped and spun, only to find myself face-to-face with Calvin. He was finally out of the sling from his shoulder injury, and back to work after medical leave during the holidays. He wore one of his usual dark suits with a black pea coat thrown over it, the wool wet with melting snow. Calvin smiled, gave my free hand a brief squeeze, then raised a takeout bag.

"What was that?" I asked the caller, still staring at Calvin. Consider me momentarily distracted. Not that I could be faulted. My new boyfriend was hot as hell and appeared to have surprised me with a lunch date. "Do you understand these are *real* antiques, though? Buy some replicas off eBay if you're going to trash them like that." I pulled the phone away and told Calvin, "She hung up on me."

"I can't imagine why."

I set the shop phone on the case. "She wanted glass buttons for a modern art installation where she—naked and covered in red paint—threw them at the wall and recited free-form poetry about her menstrual cycle and the consequences of following trends every time they shattered."

"Huh."

"But *I'm* the bad guy for trying to limit the vision of her artistry," I exclaimed.

"I brought sushi."

"You don't like sushi."

"But you do."

I took the bag and opened it, saying, "You didn't really come all this way with—yes, you did." I looked up. "Now you're just showing me up."

Calvin smiled, took my arm, and pushed me in the direction of my office. "Come sit and eat."

"It's been a busy day, though," I started to say. "I shouldn't leave Max alone."

Max snorted and spared us a look from where he stood at the counter, wrapping a trinket in tissue paper for a customer. "If I had a boyfriend who dropped by my job for lunch and nookie, I'd sure as hell be leaving you to run the shop yourself, boss."

The woman standing at the counter, waiting to pay for the sale, solemnly nodded. "Same," she agreed.

Heat crept up my neck and pooled in my cheeks. "I'm so glad I hired you," I told Max.

He shrugged. "Just keeping it real."

"Who says *nookie*, anyway?" I continued.

Calvin opened my office door and directed me inside. "There'll still be plenty of people to yell at after you've eaten."

Max laughed.

"She wanted to *break* the buttons," I protested. I put the takeout bag on the desk before adding, "And I didn't yell—"

Calvin shut the door, tugged me forward by the front of my frumpy sweater, and kissed my mouth. His lips trailed to my jaw, along the side of my neck, and then he tugged the collar of my shirt aside and bit down. I grabbed Calvin's hips to steady myself, one hand slipping inside the folds of his open coats and bumping against his shoulder holster.

"I've wanted you all day," Calvin whispered as he let up on what felt like a pretty radical hickey.

"I'm sort of gathering that."

He slid a hand between us to touch me through my trousers. "I couldn't stop thinking about sucking you off since I woke up."

I swallowed and managed, "So the sushi delivery was window dressing?"

Calvin nipped my chin as he deftly unbuttoned my pants. "The sushi is because I like you."

"Then this is dessert?"

Calvin smiled and got down on his knees—no easy task in my office, which was quite literally a converted closet. He tugged the clothes down enough to free my semi, took the head into his mouth, and groaned quietly, like I was doing *him* a favor. That reverb in the back of Calvin's throat, his hot, wet mouth, and our sudden skullduggery had me as hard as goddamn granite in no time.

Then Max knocked on the office door. "Yo, boss."

I nearly choked on my tongue, shoved Calvin back, leaned around him, and flipped the lock so I wasn't caught with my pants down in front of customers, Max, and God. "Wh-what?"

"Mr. Michaelson is here."

"Fuck me," I whispered.

Calvin smiled as he stroked my bare thighs, but refrained from commenting.

"He's here to pick up Civil War gold and silver polish," I answered.

"Cool," Max said. I listened to him take the steps beside the counter down to the showroom floor, and then his and Mr. Michaelson's voices echoed from somewhere near the Victrola.

"Want to keep going?" Calvin asked.

"I can't go out there looking like this," I hissed, pointing to my dick. "I'll put someone's eye out."

Calvin put a hand over his mouth to stifle a laugh, then took a breath and once again wrapped his lips around my cock. By age thirty-three, I'd experienced enough blowjobs to say, with absolute confidence, that Calvin's skills were next level. Not only did the man not have a gag reflex, but the way he alternated between hard and soft, fast and slow, using his lips and tongue, while the hollow of his cheeks darkened with a flush I'd now come to understand happened with little warning for someone as fair-skinned as Calvin—it was like a master class in face-fucking. And the way his freckles popped from the blush, how he rubbed at the outline of his own dick with his free hand—those were just stay-after-class-for-extra-credit details to savor.

Max knocked again. "Hey, Seb?"

"Oh my God." I put both hands on Calvin's shoulders and eased his mouth off me. "*What?*" I asked again, maybe a bit snippier this time.

There was hesitation in Max's voice as he said, "I, uh, I can't find—"

"It's in the glass display by the front window."

"All right. Thanks."

"If he knocks a third time, I'm killing him," I said.

Calvin arched one eyebrow. "It's probably not smart to be telling your detective boyfriend about your premeditated murder plot."

"If my detective boyfriend would just—just—*help me out here*, we could avoid a future of prison sentences and conjugal visits."

Calvin reached a hand up to pet my lower stomach. "Help you with what, baby?"

I swallowed audibly. "*Calvin.*"

He drew his hand down to wrap it around the base of my dick. "You mean, help you with this gorgeous cock?" Calvin looked up again.

I nodded.

"You want to say it?" he asked.

I opened my mouth, but the words were lost, like hourglass sand slipping from between my fingers. I knew he loved dirty talk, but every time I tried to return the favor, I felt like I'd *actually* die from the embarrassment. So I hesitantly shook my head.

Calvin smiled. "That's okay." He put his mouth on me again.

I grabbed the back of his head with one hand, the doorframe with the other, and just rode the incredible pleasure higher and higher until I started to peak. My balls drew up, stomach muscles clenched, and Calvin grunted as my hips jerked. "I'm close," I whispered.

"Seb?" Max interrupted—*for a third time*.

My eyes snapped open.

Calvin gripped my hips and kept sucking.

"How much is the Henry C. Doughty Gold and Silver Polish?"

"H-hundred and f-fifty," I said, sounding as if I were being strangled.

"Yeah, I told Mr. Michaelson that," Max continued, "but he says the container is priced at twenty-five cents… so he wants to pay twenty-five cents."

Calvin reached between my legs to caress my balls, and the warmth of his callused hand was what pushed me over the edge.

"Jesus Christ," I swore, my orgasm hitting me like a freight train, causing me to double over.

"Don't swear at me," Max said through the door. "*I'm* not the one who doesn't understand inflation or supply and demand."

I thrust into Calvin's mouth until the mind-numbing joy came close to pain and I was forced to push him off so that the stimulation overload didn't ruin the climax. Calvin wiped his lower lip with the pad of his thumb and then hastily unbuckled his belt. He jerked himself only a few times before biting back a groan and coming on the office floor.

I hastily righted my trousers and bent down to kiss Calvin. "I can't believe you did that," I whispered against his mouth.

"This is absolutely not a conversation you're going to have with Max after I leave."

"Not on my life."

"*Boss*," Max snapped.

"Good God, Max," I shouted.

Calvin got to his feet, made himself presentable, then turned his back as I opened the door.

I brushed past Max and walked to the register, where a stocky man—early sixties, bad comb-over—waited, rocking back and forth on the balls of his feet. "Is the year 1865, Mr. Michaelson?" I asked, sidling up to the counter.

Michaelson blinked a few times. "Uh, no, of course—"

"Then due to 150 years of inflation, and the fact that this particular artifact from the War is completely intact—no easy find as far as paper antiques are concerned—it is one hundred and fifty dollars."

Michaelson pointed at the small wooden box on the countertop. "But it's been opened."

"Yes, I suspect a Union officer likely polished his buttons and buckles with the contents."

"So then it's not mint condition."

"Nothing that was shoved into a saddlebag and used while sitting beside a campfire during a war is going to be mint," I growled.

"I won't pay one fifty," Michaelson protested, voice growing shrill.

"Fine. One forty-nine and seventy-five cents."

Michaelson slapped the palm of his hand on the counter. "I won't ever shop here again!" he declared before stomping toward the front door.

"*Good,*" I called after him, leaning forward on the counter to watch him go. "We deal and sell in antiques, sir. Those cost *money.*" The door slammed shut and the overhead bell rattled obnoxiously. "I have rent and employee health insurance to pay for!" I continued, even though Michaelson was long gone.

Calvin appeared just then, leaned between Max and me, and set the container of assorted sushi in front of me. He put a pair of disposable chopsticks on top, then said, "Before your low blood sugar scares off any more customers."

"Twenty-five cents," I said with a snort, grabbing the chopsticks and yanking them apart. They didn't snap evenly. "This paper's still got color, right?" I asked next, directing the question at Max while pointing at the box with the chopsticks.

He obediently nodded. "Yup. A bright orange."

"Intact paper, text still legible, and showing no overt discoloration from sunlight exposure or age. And he wanted to spend…. I mean, the buying power of a quarter alone nowadays—"

Calvin nodded, took my chin, and gave me a chaste kiss. "I know. Eat your lunch."

"Fine."

"I'll call you."

"You can just come over tonight," I suggested instead.

Calvin smiled. "I'll see what I can do."

After he had said goodbye and seen himself out, Max said without any prompting, "Aren't blowjobs supposed to put you in a better mood?"

I had a mouthful of salmon and rice, so I didn't say anything. I merely picked up my food and returned to the office.

Max made a slurping noise in my wake.

CREDIT SCORES AND COHABITATION

—

After *The Mystery of the Curiosities*
POV: Sebastian Snow

—

After the events of the Curiosities case—most importantly, the part where former flatfoots Lowry and Brigg planted a homemade explosive device in my building and *blew it up*—I'd been crashing at Calvin's too-small-for-two studio and surfing Pop's couch for nearly two months.

Which was two months too long, if you asked me. *Not* that I wasn't grateful. If I hadn't had either of them to provide a roof over my head, I'd have probably racked up an unbelievable hotel bill, a debt I wouldn't have been able to afford, while I'd spent every spare moment I had on what seemed to be a totally fruitless search for a new apartment.

But, I mean, minus the hotel-debt part, that was the exact situation I was in. Which sounded nuts. I lived in New York City, a place that nearly nine million called home. How on God's green Earth could I not find a new apartment?

Heh. *Well*. There's a reason Pop hadn't moved in forty years.

The rental market in this city was so absurd that once you managed to plant your flag in a kingdom to call your own, it'd take an *actual bomb* to make you give it up. Realtors and brokers were always looking for the wealthiest potential client, so for your average Joe like me, who just wanted a decent apartment in Manhattan and not some multimillion-dollar penthouse on the Upper West Side, they tended to run the gamut of shady, rude, condescending, or outright noncommunicative.

And with the trust-fund babies moving to the East Coast, rent was shooting into the stratosphere, which made searching for an apartment for two without breaking the bank even trickier. Although, Calvin's preferences regarding apartments were shockingly little, which sort of explained why he'd been content to live in that closet-sized studio for half a decade.

Pet-friendly.

Laundry in building would "be nice."

And… that was it.

Me, on the other hand, being the neurotic asshole that I was, really struggled with change. I was dead set on finding a place in the East Village so I could still walk to and from the Emporium every day. A walk-up or multiuse—nothing with elevators or doormen. No ground floor apartments either. They got too warm in the winter with the way water radiators tended to disproportionately heat the building, and I refused to listen to the *bang* of the front door as tenants came and went at all hours. And no laundry in-building was an automatic no for me. A do not pass go, do not collect two hundred dollars kind of no. I was *not* schlepping our clothes to the laundromat every week.

Anyway. I knew my own requirements would shrink the pool of eligible rentals, but the last two months had been nothing but surreal disappointment. And a lot of real estate agents didn't like working with sole proprietors either—extra paperwork for them. So they'd simply tell me our combined income wasn't what the landlord was looking for, which was the biggest steaming turd of a lie someone has ever had the gall to say to my face. Then there was the one Realtor who had stood me up on multiple viewings that I'd spent hours organizing. And yet another who had showed us a place we were totally in love with, only to rent it to some suit before our credit scores had even checked out. I'd reached rage-tears level of upset after that one, and even Calvin reamed the agent's ass over the phone when we realized what had happened.

Apartment hunting in New York sucked.

"What're your plans tomorrow, kiddo?" Pop asked, bringing our plates to the sink.

I was scrubbing the pan I'd cooked dinner in and said with a shrug, "The same thing I do every Monday. Line up apartments viewings during the day and then cry into a pint of ice cream at night."

"I know you really want to stick to your old neighborhood," Pop began, "but at this point, maybe expanding the search radius would be for the best."

"Someone has to die sooner or later."

"Sebastian."

I huffed and scrubbed harder. "There's lots of apartments in the East Village. It's just… there's something fucking stupid about each of them."

"I think you're being a little picky."

"No, Dad. I'm not." I pointed the brush at him. "The place

I saw this morning was above a pizza shop. It was about nine hundred degrees inside because of the brick ovens, smelled like day-old marinara, and I swear to God every resident was a college freshman. I don't want to be the only adult in the building."

"All right, fair, I wouldn't want to live there either."

"And I'm entirely convinced the place on Avenue A is owned by the mob."

"Now you're exaggerating."

"As the Realtor was showing me the kitchen, I could hear the guy upstairs screaming about Tony owing him 'his fuckin' money.' He doesn't strike me as the kind of neighbor who would appreciate living in close quarters to a cop, and I don't want Calvin or I wearing cement shoes."

Pop sighed.

I rinsed the pan, picked up the hand towel, and dried it off. "I really liked the place on Thirteenth Street, but that asshole landlord came *this close* to saying gays need not apply, and I'm not paying rent to someone like that."

Pop patted my shoulder. "I agree—"

"See? There's something wrong with all of them. But the East Village is the ideal location," I continued. "I can walk to your place and to work. You know I avoid the subway like the plague. Plus, it's a convenient drive for Calvin to get to his precinct. I'll have to keep a constant supply of Ben & Jerry's around until I finally land a lease."

My cell started ringing from the dining table.

Pop walked across the room, fetched my phone, and helped himself to answering the call, which meant it was either Max or Calvin. And on a Sunday evening, it wouldn't be Max. "Hello, Calvin! How're you doing? … Hm-hm…. I bet. We just finished dinner, actually. Let me see if Sebastian is available."

"I'm right here," I stated, holding my hands out, like, *What gives?*

"I've got the caramel chocolate cheesecake, actually," Pop told Calvin, chuckling under his breath.

I turned, opened the freezer to my left, and pulled out a pint of what looked to be the best damn ice cream those two crazy Vermonters had ever thought up.

"After being his father for thirty-three years, I've picked up a trick or two," Pop concluded. "All right. You be safe." He lowered the phone from his ear and asked, "Did you want to talk to your boyfriend?"

"Well, he called me, Dad," I said, grabbing for the phone.

Pop held it out of reach. "Are you going to tone down the dramatics?"

"Jesus Christ—"

"Sebastian."

"Fine. All right. I won't lament about being homeless to the man whose job it is to put up with my whining." I swiped the phone, gave Pop a leveled look, and said while bringing it to my ear, "Sebastian speaking on Sebastian's phone."

"It's my job to put up with your whining?" Calvin asked.

I felt my face heat and said, "No. I mean—but sometimes it's nice to, uh—"

Calvin laughed, his voice deep and rich. It always had a way of being soothing, maybe because he never laughed *at* me, but instead, with me. "Are you looking for comfort or solutions, baby?"

"Comfort."

"Then bitch away."

"I would, but my dad is watching me."

Pop rolled his eyes, let out another one of those long-suffering sighs, and went to collect Maggie's leash for her evening constitutional.

"Quinn stepped out for a smoke," Calvin was saying, "so I thought I'd call you."

"Aww."

"I know." The distinct hum of a water fountain cooler kicked on in the background. Calvin must have been walking down one of the hallways of his precinct. "Tell me about this morning's viewing…. Was it on Stuyvesant?"

"Ninth."

"How was it?"

"Stinky and prepubescent."

Calvin was quiet for a moment, then concluded with, "So no."

"No." I leaned against the counter and gave Pop a small wave when he and Maggie left the apartment. "I talked to a new real estate agent today. He's going to show me a few places tomorrow."

"I'll go with you."

"Really?"

"You've done most of the work so far," Calvin said. "I can manage a few viewings."

"I meant more—really, you have tomorrow off."

"I do."

"Oh."

"Although, my sergeant won't mind some over—"

"Nice try."

I could hear Calvin's smile as he asked, "Can I take you out for breakfast tomorrow?"

I shut the passenger door of Calvin's car and stared at a six-story walk-up, its façade a light-colored stone, and the texture reminiscent of the Queen Anne architecture that still dotted the city. "It's a dumbbell tenement," I stated.

"It's what?" Calvin asked, moving around the front of the car and joining me on the sidewalk.

"I did a little digging on the address. It was built in 1890, so it's considered part of the Old Law Tenement Act. The structure of the buildings cinch in the middle to create an air corridor. Hence the nickname, dumbbell."

"Is that good or bad?"

"Good," I said, pushing my sunglasses up and looking at Calvin. "I mean, I told Mr. Thomas we were looking for one-bedroom, pet-friendly places, and he gave me this address."

"Seems like a nice place."

"And no greasy dollar slices on the first floor."

"You like the dollar slices."

"To eat. I don't want to *live* in a pizza shop."

"Sebastian Snow?"

We both looked to the front door as a man hurried down the steps, a smile on his face far too bright and cheery for just a little after eight in the morning.

"That's me," I said, barely having raised my hand in acknowledgment before he grabbed it and pumped enthusiastically.

"Timothy Thomas, Realtor. We talked on the phone yesterday."

"Right." He was still shaking my hand.

"You can call me Timothy. Or Thomas. But *not* Timmy Tom!" He laughed—loudly.

I extracted my hand from his and said, "Timothy. This is my partner, Calvin Winter—"

Timothy was already trying to dislocate Calvin's arm before I'd finished with introductions. "As we say in the real estate business, it's a *real* pleasure. Will you be joining us today?”

“That’s the plan,” Calvin answered.

“Then let’s go find your next dream home, gentlemen.” Timothy waved for us to follow him to the door.

I turned and started for the car.

Calvin grabbed my arm, spun me around, and pushed me forward.

“I don’t think I have the strength.”

“Yes, you do.”

“He made a real estate pun.”

“Come on, sweetheart.”

I never did have the willpower to argue with Calvin when he used his terms of endearment on me.

I stepped into the vestibule, and we followed Timothy past the bank of mailboxes on the wall and down a short hallway, but when he reached the stairs, Timothy bypassed them, brought us around the backside, and started down the flight leading to the basement.

“You’ll love this place,” Timothy said over his shoulder. “Recently renovated, all-new kitchen appliances. You have a dog, right? Access to the backyard is restricted to the tenants of B1.”

“Timothy,” I said as we reached the landing. “I was really firm about the no-first-floor-apartments thing.”

He unlocked the door to the unit, flipped a light switch on the wall, and said, “This isn’t the first floor! It’s the basement.”

I turned to look up at Calvin. “Please don’t make me,” I whispered.

“Take a quick peek before saying no.”

“I’m not a nice person.”

“Pretend you are.” Calvin leaned down to kiss the side of my head.

The apartment might have been okay—never mind I wouldn't live in a basement regardless—but more in the sense that it'd have been easy on my eyes. Except during the renovation Timothy had mentioned, it seemed like they'd installed no less than a thousand recessed lights, all pumped to maximum wattage, and I could barely make out the shape of the kitchen island, let alone any details like the floor tile or potential for crown molding.

"I can't," I said, shielding the tops of my sunglasses with a hand. "Sorry. It's—"

From behind me was a dull *thud*, followed by a hiss and murmured curse.

I turned to see Calvin rubbing the top of his head. I glanced up at the ceiling, then asked, "Did you hit your head?"

"We're going to need a taller place, Timothy," Calvin said from the doorway.

As it turned out, the too-short basement really set the tone for the rest of the day.

Timothy showed us a railroad-style apartment, which he insisted was the same square footage as a "normal" one-bedroom, with the trade-off being it was four feet wide—the only way we'd fit a bed in the back was if it were folded like a taco, and I was likely to begin suffering from a mild case of claustrophobia. But hey, it was so long, we could throw Dillon's Frisbee from the kitchen to the bedroom with ease and not even *have* to go to the dog park.

The third apartment was in the process of being gutted and renovated, which I was fine with since I could imagine the end result, but the plumbing was already installed for the tub, and the tub was beside the oven. When I asked Timothy where the tub was *actually* going to be located, because I wasn't interested in being able to soak in the bath and check on dinner at the same time, he pursed his lips and suggested we look at the next unit on his list.

Number four turned out to be a modern loft, the bedroom being accessible only by ladder. I knew how that'd pan out for me too. First week—stumbling out of bed, blind and bleary-eyed—trip on a rung, break my neck, and end up dead on the kitchen floor. But even more important than my neck was the fact that Dillon needed access to Calvin during the night. The dog had really zeroed-in on Calvin's sleep patterns over the last month, and in the event that a nightmare awoke him, Dillon seemed to always be there, waiting. And he was able to calm Calvin down a lot faster than I could. So the trendy loft was another big fat *no*.

That's when Timothy uttered the word that ended our brief tryst. "Midtown."

I looked at him. "What?"

"I have a great place in Midtown. Forty-third and Sixth—"

"That's Times Square."

Timothy made a so-so motion with one hand. "It's a block away."

"I think we have to break up, Timothy," I said solemnly.

"I'm going to have to turn to Craigslist."

"No situation is that dire," Calvin said, shuffling around his apartment, locking the door and turning out the lights for the night.

I scooted to make room on his bed, my back pressed up against the exposed bare brick. "In two months we've seen every dump, shithole, funhouse, and OSHA violation in the entire East Village."

"311."

"What?"

Calvin pulled the blankets back and got in bed. "OSHA

is workplace health and safety. I believe that in the city, you report private residences to NYC311."

"But my point is, these apartments were *with* the help of a Realtor. You make good money. I make decent money. We're both established at our jobs." I'd started to twine my leg with Calvin's but froze. "You don't have debilitating credit, do you? I know I'm paying off student loans, but it's still considered a good score."

"It's something like 810."

"*Something like?*"

"I haven't checked it lately, but I know it won't hinder us."

I dragged my hand through Calvin's chest hair. "You've got near-perfect credit and we're still pretending we can share a twin-size bed."

"Be patient. We'll find a place."

"You don't know that," I grumbled.

"Statistics and probability," Calvin continued. "Eventually those will weigh in our favor." He put his hand on the back of my head. "Did you really want to keep talking about this?"

"You want to go to sleep?"

In the glow of light pollution that filtered in through the window at the foot of the bed, I could see Calvin's eyebrows slowly creep to his hairline. "No… but I haven't seen you in a few days. I thought we could fuck first and talk later?"

That was one way to bring my gripefest to a screeching halt.

"Seb?"

"Huh?"

"You okay?"

"Oh. Yeah. It's just—my dick got hard so fast, the blood stopped pumping to my brain for a second."

Calvin laughed. He wrapped his big arms around me, rolled me onto my back, and kissed me until I saw nothing but stars.

Dillon stuck his wet nose in my face and snuffled loudly. I grunted and gave the dog a shove. Calvin's voice was quiet as he called Dillon, who, in turn, smacked my face with his tail, then jumped off the bed.

I groped for Calvin's pillow, tugged it to my chest, and inhaled whispers of his spicy cologne that lingered on the fabric. "Where'd you go?" I managed to ask without sounding completely drunk on sleep.

"I had to take Dillon out."

"Hmm."

"Do you want coffee?" Calvin asked.

"Sure," I answered, sort of slurring that word a little.

"Then get dressed."

"No, thanks."

I could hear Calvin's smile as he added, "I haven't gone shopping. We can stop at Starbucks before you go to the Emporium."

I raised my head and stared at Calvin's gray, blurry form hovering in the pseudokitchen. "I'm thinking of calling out. Luckily, I'm the boss and I can do that sort of thing."

"Do you not feel well?" Calvin was walking toward me now.

"I'm fine. But the postcoital hangover is still going strong."

Calvin put a knee on the mattress and leaned over me. He was staring, an expectant sort of expression on his face.

"I've got a burn in muscles I didn't even know I had," I

explained.

"Oh yeah?"

"And I don't think I've ever…." I trailed off when Calvin's eyes seemed to glimmer with sudden arousal.

"Ever, what?"

"You know."

"Do I?"

I could feel heat prickling my face now. "The thing I did."

"You mean, come without touching yourself?"

I swallowed hard and nodded. "That'd be the thing, yes."

Calvin ran one hand down my bare back, slipped it under the covers, and firmly grabbed one asscheek. "You know what I want?" he asked, dropping his voice low.

"It's really not taking much imagination on my part."

His mouth quirked into an unbelievably sexy grin before Calvin leaned close and whispered, "I want you to get up so I can have coffee." Then he smacked my ass hard and stood from the bed.

I sat on my knees in a rush, shouting, "*Calvin!*"

"That's my name, baby."

I rubbed my ass with one hand and reached for my glasses on the nightstand with the other. "Be gentle." I climbed out of bed and went to his closet, where I'd been keeping a few articles of clothing, since spending the night was usually a spur-of-the-moment decision.

Calvin wrapped his arms around me from behind and kissed my neck. "That's not what you said last night."

I'd gone from being sexual putty in bed to wanting to melt into the floorboards from humiliation in a snap. How'd Calvin do this? Talk sexy or dirty without even trying, without caring? And here I was, ready to spontaneously combust from the utter embarrassment of admitting—in broad daylight, no less—that I liked having my ass spanked.

I shrugged, cleared my throat, and tried to say with a casualness I didn't feel, "Sort of think different when you've already got a chub." I grabbed a pair of trousers and a button-down shirt I'd left folded, so now it had wrinkles on the front.

Calvin stepped to the side and gently turned me to look at him. He held my face in both hands and gave my lips a chaste kiss. "Good morning."

"Morning."

"I like you."

I couldn't help but smile then. Calvin had proven to be a really intuitive partner from the start, but especially where sex was concerned. He was always keyed in to how close I was, or what got me off, or what I wanted but refused to ask for, so of course he put two and two together pretty quickly and realized that I was about to spiral into panic over sounding like a complete weirdo for enjoying something so— "I like you too," I said. This perfect man was honest to God willing and wanting to live under the same roof as me and my neurosis. What had I done to deserve this?

Calvin gave my jaw a brief rub with the pad of his thumb, my whiskers pleasantly scraping back and forth. "There's a grande house brew with your name on it just waiting."

"All right, all right."

"And a cheese danish, if they haven't run out."

"Now you're singing my song."

Dressed and as ready for Tuesday as I could hope to be, we left with Dillon and made a pit stop at the Starbucks two blocks from Calvin's studio. I ran inside to pick up our coffees and came back out with a cup in either hand, trying to push my sunglasses up my nose, which only resulted in me sloshing a few drops of scalding-hot house brew on my hand. Calvin, waiting with Dillon beside a USPS mailbox, took his latte and nudged my glasses up with his finger.

"Thanks," I said before sucking on my hand where the coffee had burned me.

"No danish?"

"They only had scones left." I wrapped a hand around Calvin's bicep, and we started walking again. I didn't need to be at the Emporium for another half hour, so we zigzagged around the neighborhood for a time—down one street, across an avenue, down the next street, across another avenue. It was nice. Being punted back and forth between Calvin's place and Pop's like a football meant our already vastly different work schedules aligned even less than usual. So when I managed to grab free time with Calvin, being together to enjoy coffee and watch the city wake up for its morning hustle—it was something to cherish.

Dillon stopped to read the doggy correspondence on a tree, and as he did his thing, I shielded the tops of my sunglasses to study the street of historical tenements, all beautifully restored—a mixture of walk-ups and multiuse buildings that had shops on the ground floor.

"Maybe we should consider Brooklyn," I said at length.

Calvin sipped his coffee and looked at me. "You don't want to live in Brooklyn."

"No. I definitely don't. But Max has been trying to convince me to move out there since February."

"Max wants a buddy to hang out with."

I raised an eyebrow. "I've got a decade on Max."

"You're still his friend."

"Because I pay him and provide health insurance."

Calvin shook his head but was smiling as he pulled me close enough to kiss my forehead. "Keep telling yourself that." Stepping back, he looked over his shoulder to the cross streets we'd just passed. He plucked the empty cup from my hand and said, "I'm going to toss these real quick."

As soon as Calvin backtracked to the trash cans on the corner, a woman in a smart business suit stormed out of the side door that provided access to apartments above what looked like an expensive café and some kind of frumpy tie-dye shop—because *East Village*. She was obviously upset, with a death-grip on a cell in one hand while she shoved her perfectly curled dark hair away from her face with the other. She stormed by me to the curb and waved for a taxi, but it was occupied and kept driving. I recognized the look on her face as she stomped a foot. She was close to rage-crying. There was nothing I hated more than a woman so upset that she had to cry in order to keep herself from throttling someone.

"Ma'am?" I spoke up.

She spun to face me. "Mr. Stevenson?"

I held both hands up like I were trying to defend my innocence. "No."

She rolled her eyes and checked her phone again.

"I, uh… I won't insult you by asking if you're okay…."

She shoved the phone into the purse slung over one shoulder, then turned and pointed at the building she'd exited. "I woke up at the asscrack of dawn to show this apartment to that entitled shit." She turned her gaze on me. "Do you have any idea how long it takes to do my hair?"

"Probably a long time," I answered.

"An *hour*," she retorted.

"It's very pretty."

Her shoulders came down about an inch from her ears. "…Thanks."

"Sure."

"I had to come in from Queens for this," she continued, growing agitated all over again. "This is the third client to blow me off. They have my phone number! They can't text? Are their fingers broken? The owner is going to pull this unit from me if I can't rent it, and if I have no properties, I'll never get paid, and then what the hell was the point of getting my real estate license and moving to this city?" She directed her index finger at me this time. "Explain *that*. God, I *hate* tenants." Then, realizing what she'd said aloud, she hastily added, "I didn't mean—"

"It's okay," I told her. "I hate Realtors."

For some reason that bit of honesty caused a smile to split her face, and then she laughed a bright and happy laugh. "This industry is bonkers."

"No kidding."

"I'm so sorry. I can't believe I just had a meltdown on the street in front of a stranger."

"It's New York." I offered a hand. "Sebastian Snow."

"Joyce Kelly," she said, shaking it.

I eyed the multiuse briefly, then asked, "So what's the place Mr. Stevenson missed out on?"

"A loft."

"Oh. Ladder?"

Joyce seemed confused for a beat, but then her expression shifted. "No, no. The bedroom and full bath are accessible by stairs."

"What's, um… what's downstairs?"

"A living room and separate kitchen."

"What floor?"

Joyce was beginning to look skeptical. "Fourth," she drew out. "Why?"

"Rental or purchase?"

"A rental—sorry, are you—?"

"What's it going for?"

She blinked almost comically before opening her huge purse and taking out a manila folder. "I'm brand stinkin' new to New York," she explained, opening the file and offering me the printouts. "I carry these little cheat sheets with me. It has all the information about the neighborhood, building, and unit."

I held the file close to my face so I didn't have to dig out the magnifying glass from my messenger bag. The provided photos were of a huge apartment with high ceilings, big windows, nice floors and walls—must have been recently renovated. I studied the bullet points underneath the pictures. "There's a live-in super, laundry in-building, pet-friendly—" I did a double take at the monthly price, then looked at Joyce. "Is this a joke?"

"What do you mean?"

"This price is real?"

"Yes? I mean, tenants have to pay internet, gas, and electricity. Plus, there's first and last month's rent, as well as a security fee."

"What's your fee?" I countered, waiting for the other shoe to drop.

"The owner has agreed to pay my broker fee. Assuming I ever get the damn place rented."

"Did someone die in there?" I asked, handing Joyce her folder back.

"Why would you ask that?"

"I'm trying to figure out why it's still readily available."

She shrugged. "Your guess is as good as mine. I think it's a great place."

"Can I view it?" I blurted out.

Joyce startled. "R-really? But I—"

"Sebastian?"

I turned as Calvin and Dillon were returning from the corner. I reached a hand out for him while saying, "Hey, there's a loft on the fourth floor that's available, and Joyce

Kelly, Realtor Extraordinaire, had a viewing cancellation." To Joyce I said, "This is my partner, Calvin Winter. He's a detective with the NYPD. I own a business a few blocks from here. We have savings and great credit. What do you say?"

"Uh… well, you'd have to fill out an application," she began, giving us a wary look, like she was expecting to be punk'd at any minute.

"We'd be happy to," Calvin said, quick to take my lead when he realized how excited I was.

"Provide proof of income," Joyce continued, ticking the points off on her fingers. "Plus, we'll need to run a credit check."

I nodded like a bobblehead. "Not a problem. We've been looking for two months—I've got the routine down pat."

Joyce hesitated, tugged on a hoop earring, and chewed her lower lip.

"You came all the way from Queens," I reminded her.

She made a *tsk* sound under her breath. "That's right. Okay. Let's do it." Joyce smiled, unearthed the keys from her purse, and led the way to the front door.

I murmured the monthly rent to Calvin as we followed her inside.

"Your half would be more than your old place," he whispered. "Can you afford that?"

"I'll shop at Goodwill again." I plucked at the shirt I had on and added, "This was eighty bucks at Nordstrom. And that was its *on sale* price."

As we hiked the stairs, Calvin said, his voice just loud enough to be heard over the creak of old steps, "I think you look sexy in a slim fit."

I cleared my throat and said over my shoulder, "Maybe I can find another way to save money."

When we reached the fourth floor, Joyce said, "Here we

are—4B." She unlocked the door and flicked the lights on. "What do you think?"

I cautiously stepped into the apartment.

And it felt as if I'd come home.

THE GHOST OF DURANGO

—

Before *The Mystery of the Moving Image*
POV: Sebastian Snow

—

It'd finally happened.

Despite my nonstop protestations and lamentations to the contrary.

I was on my first-ever vacation.

And not the sort where I could still do research, write emails, and make calls on behalf of the Emporium. A staycation, I believe those were called. *Oh no.* This was a real pack-your-toothbrush-and-clean-underwear, we're-outta-here sort of vacation.

I will admit… it'd been *a year*. And it was only April.

Murder and mystery seemed to be behind us for good, and Calvin and I finally had an apartment—a gorgeously renovated loft on the top floor of a multiuse in the East Village—which I'd nearly lost my mind in the pursuit of. (If it'd taken even one day more, I'd have gone feral and ended up in Central Park, throwing bread crumbs at myself while trying to live as the most dominant pigeon of Frisbee Hill.) The one downfall to our new digs was that the landlord didn't want the lease starting until the first week of May. So instead of sitting on our thumbs, Calvin had gone ahead and said the one thing I hated hearing more than sugar-free cheesecake.

"I need a vacation."

By *I*, he meant *we*, of course, because when you share utility bills with a guy, you're sort of a packaged deal. I'd immediately declined. Small-business owner and all that. And I don't know if Calvin slipped Max and my dad a twenty or something, but I was out-voted—three to one—on the matter. I did, in fact, need a vacation. Was, in fact, expected to accompany my boyfriend. And no, in fact, was not staying in the state of New York.

That's how I also ended up taking my very first flight at thirty-three years old. I left from LaGuardia with nothing but Calvin, our checked suitcase, and copious dread bubbling in my gut.

Our destination?

Denver International.

Why?

Not a clue. Calvin said it was a surprise. If I hadn't been such a tweaked-out ball of anxiety on the cab ride to the airport, through security, when I was pulled aside because the officer wanted to inspect my cane—then *me*, when I told her to swab it down for GSR—boarding, and turbulence that had me white-knuckling Calvin's hand the rest of the flight, I might have swooned that my man was bringing me on a romantic adventure.

Although, Denver was not what I thought of when riding off into the sunset.

After we'd landed in the Mile High City and briefly detoured to the bathrooms because I had a bloody nose from the altitude, we'd stopped at a rental counter in the baggage claim area and Calvin was given keys to a car he'd apparently organized for us prior to leaving New York. Then, once we'd been driving for the better part of the afternoon, stopping briefly for lunch at a rustic, frontier-style restaurant that boasted a menu of entirely local ingredients and game and was nothing short of *incredible*, again for gas, and then for a photo op at a national park, like real tourists, I'd come to the logical conclusion that we weren't staying anywhere near Denver.

"Cal."

"Seb."

"Please, for the love of God, tell me where we're going. My ass fell asleep fifty miles ago."

"Our destination won't make any difference to your ass."

"Are we going to New Mexico?"

"Not quite."

I tugged my phone from my pocket.

"Who're you texting?" Calvin asked, not looking away from the road.

"Max."

He swiped the cell and tucked it between his legs. "Let Max work," Calvin said. "You've checked in with him half a dozen times already."

"What if he can't find the price of an antique?"

"Then he'll call you."

"What if there's a fire?"

"He'll call 911."

"What if—?"

"Baby, I need you to relax, okay?"

I slumped in my seat, but after a minute or two, held my hand out. "Can I have my phone back?"

"Why?"

I motioned to the radio. "I want to look up this band."

"Jefferson Airplane."

"I want to look up the song."

"'Somebody to Love.'"

"Calvin, give me my phone!"

He held it out, saying, "If you text Max, I'll find out, and you'll be in trouble. Understand?"

I grumbled a response, took the phone, and shoved it in my pocket. I studied Calvin from behind my shades as he put his hand back on the wheel. I so rarely saw him in jeans and a T-shirt that each time it was a vivid reminder of his Superman physique. Not that I didn't see it plenty in the bedroom, but there was something so satisfying in the way his thighs filled out a pair of Levi's, or how the sleeves of his shirt always bulged from his biceps. And the constellations of freckles smattering his bare arms? That was icing on the cake.

Sunglasses met sunglasses, and Calvin asked, "What?"

I shrugged. "Enjoying the view."

Calvin looked out the windshield, a smile tugging at the corner of his mouth. "The mountains are nice."

"There're mountains?" I turned my head. "Oh. Would you look at that."

It wasn't much longer before Calvin made a turn for what a sign indicated to be the direction of Durango. Mom-and-pop shops began cropping up along the sides of the road, just far enough outside the heart of the city that rent was undoubtedly cheaper, but the trade-off being tourists were very unlikely to poke their heads in. Locals' shopping only. We passed no fewer than a dozen different lodgings—questionable motels, empty parking lots glowing in the late-afternoon desert sun, low-star chain hotels, family-owned B&Bs—but Calvin didn't stop driving.

"Are we… going to the Main Avenue Historic District?" I finally asked.

"I knew you'd figure it out."

I sat up at attention. "Are we really?"

"You know about it?"

"It cuts through downtown Durango. There's something like eighty buildings of historic significance that're included. It's near the Durango & Silverton Narrow Gauge Railroad too."

"Is it?"

"Yeah. It's a passenger line for sightseeing now, but it was originally both passenger and freight, moving ore from the surrounding mines in the 18—you knew this."

"I didn't," Calvin said with a chuckle.

"Yes, you did. You have tells."

"I do?"

"When you rub your chin like that."

"I knew there was a railroad," he corrected.

I narrowed my eyes. "How'd you know?"

"What do you mean?"

"*I* know because Durango is a famous Wild West town, founded in 1881, that wisely preserved its history for weirdos like me."

"You're not a weirdo."

For some reason that assurance in Calvin's tone made me blush. "Er—well, that's why I know about the railroad. How do *you* know?"

Calvin didn't answer until he'd rounded a corner and came on to an absolutely pristine street of historical buildings and quaint boutique shops. He parked on the side of the road outside a grand four-story brick building, turned the ignition off, then pointed out my window. "I know because I booked us a ride on the railroad through the Strater."

I gave Calvin a quick glance, but my hand was already on the door handle, and then I was opening it and scrambling to my feet. I stared up at the famous hotel and once social hotspot of Colorado, almost in disbelief, but nope—there was the sign over the front door.

THE STRATER HOTEL

Calvin shut the driver's door and came around the front of the car. "Seb?"

"We're staying here for the week?"

"Yup." Calvin put a hand on my back and rubbed small circles. "You okay?"

"Because… it's closer to tourist sites?"

Calvin nodded slowly. "That, sure. And because I thought you might enjoy a Victorian hotel more than the Holiday Inn. What's wrong?"

Shaking my head, I hastily said, "No, nothing." I put a hand on the back of Calvin's neck and pulled him down into a kiss. "Thank you. This is amazing."

"Worth the drive?"

I laughed quietly. "I take back any and all complaints." I kissed Calvin again.

"Do you *mind*?"

We both turned toward the steps at the same time. A woman, closer to Calvin's age, stood just outside the front doors, one hand on a toddler trying to escape her grasp, the other on her hip, striking a true Mom Pose. Behind her, a completely mortified teenage boy was holding his phone and gaping at his mom through a curtain of long, stringy hair. A third kid was a few feet away, arms wrapped around a parking meter, swinging back and forth, completely oblivious to Mommy Dearest's conniption.

"Do you *mind*?" Mommy repeated, pressing on that final word even more than the first time.

Now, I know I'm the last person who should form opinions based on another's sense of fashion, but the pleated capris, tucked-in blouse buttoned to her throat, and carefully placed pearl necklace under the collar—honey was fresh out of her white picket fence suburbia.

"Ma'am?" Calvin asked politely.

"There are children here," she hissed.

"*Mom*," the teen tried.

"Hush, Jeremy!" She wrangled her toddler again, and the kid started crying. "You've made Aaron cry," Mommy said accusingly, very much at us and not Jeremy.

I kept my hand wrapped around Calvin and said, "I think he's crying because he's got a load in his drawers and a face sticky with snot."

"If I wanted to see—" She struggled a beat before spitting out, like the words tasted bad, "—*gay sex*, I'd rent that on pay-per-view."

"And if I wanted to see kids licking parking meters," I said calmly, "I'd go to the zoo."

Mommy's expression twisted like a corkscrew. She looked to her right, then left, and saw the middle child was, indeed, now licking the meter she'd been swinging from. "Mandy! You don't know where that's been!" She dragged the toddler behind her, grabbed Mandy with her other hand, and hoofed it down the sidewalk. "Jeremy!" She snapped over her shoulder.

Jeremy was smirking as he reluctantly followed at a distance.

"That was pretty good," Calvin stated, looking down at me.

"Thanks. Is pay-per-view even a thing anymore?"

"I have no idea. Let's check in."

The interior of the hotel was exactly what I'd hoped for—eclectic and beautiful Victorian furniture, vivid period wallpaper, and dark woodwork, all merging with a touch of upper-class Western aesthetic. There was a sitting area near the plate-glass window on the left and a grand reception desk immediately ahead. A hall just to the right looked to lead to the staircase.

"Henry Strater built the hotel in 1887," I was saying to Calvin as he approached the desk. "It cost seventy thousand dollars at the time. He leased it to H.L. Rice to manage, and there ended up being a falling-out between them. So he built another hotel to compete with the Strater."

"The Columbian," answered the handsome, probably blond, gentleman at the counter. "Right next door, if you can believe it. You know your Strater history, sir."

"I have a complicated relationship with the nineteenth century."

That made Calvin laugh under his breath before he said, "We're checking in. Reservation is under Calvin Winter."

Blondie tip-tapped on his keyboard, glanced up every few click-clacks, then said, "Five nights, a deluxe king. Is that correct?"

Calvin nodded and confirmed his credit card on file.

Blondie was passing Calvin a set of room keys as he said, "If you step just outside the Strater, Mahogany Grille is to your right—it's a very relaxed and romantic setting for dinner. The menus are sourced from local farms and ranches.

And to the left is the Diamond Belle, if you'd like to grab a drink and enjoy some live music." He looked directly at me. "The saloon girls are in costume, for the nineteenth century connoisseurs."

"My tastes are more in-line with cowboys."

Blondie smiled and winked. "We've got those too."

Calvin took our suitcase in one hand and nudged me. "Let's go, baby."

"He winked at me," I stage-whispered by the time we'd reached the wide staircase and started up the steps.

"Uh-huh."

"Men don't wink at me."

"That one did."

"He must have had something in his eye."

"Maybe he's also a connoisseur."

I stopped at the second-floor landing, but Calvin moved around me and started up the next set of stairs. "You're using that you're-not-property-but-I'm-still-territorial voice."

Calvin paused and looked over his shoulder at me.

I shrugged and climbed past him. "It's hot." I managed not to shiver when Calvin lightly drew his free hand down my spine and to the small of my back. At the third floor, I let Calvin take the lead, since he had the key cards. "Was there a reason for Durango in particular?"

He scanned the card and pushed the door to our room open. "A CSU detective I'm friendly with got married here last month. She told me about the hotel and local attractions—" Calvin paused to push the suitcase against the wall, turned, and flashed me a handsome, lopsided smile. "It made me think of you."

I scratched my scruff with one hand and said, a little self-consciously, while stepping inside, "You're getting so lucky tonight." I studied an armoire in the far corner, a squat dresser with an attached mirror, and a set of mismatched chairs. I ran my hand along the blanket on the bed and the footboard, which looked like hand-carved mahogany, then moved to peer through the curtains at the bay window. "Beautiful view of Main Avenue." I perked at the distant sound of a whistle and turned to Calvin. "You can hear the train from here."

He had his arms crossed and was leaning against the open door with a very satisfied expression on his face.

I pointed up. "They've even got the ceiling paper."

Calvin inclined his head toward the hall. "Let's get something to eat."

I started back toward the door, but paused at the dresser to pick up a booklet. I flipped to a random page. It was a journal of some sort, messages written from plenty of past guests. I brought it close and squinted, but no joy. I needed my magnifying glass. I went to Calvin and offered it.

He didn't question me while accepting the journal. Calvin had been learning how to react to my need for help with situations that the rest of the world considered inconsequential, but for me, were at times akin to moving mountains. Calvin was also learning that he was one of the few people I trusted, one of the few I could admit to not having an adaptation for every situation, and that maybe I couldn't hurdle this issue alone. My entire life, well-meaning strangers had this way of pitying me, of making me feel less or stupid or—or like I couldn't actually fucking read and they were performing a goddamn mitzvah on my behalf.

I was a smart man.

I just had shitty eyesight and sometimes needed a little assistance.

Calvin turned a few pages and then hummed in response to a self-realization. "This must be the ghost diary."

"Of course it is."

He was smiling as he looked up from the pages.

"Catherine—the detective—"

"The married one."

"The married one. She said all of the rooms have these. If something spooky happens, you're supposed to record the event for future guests to read."

"The hotel is haunted," I asked flatly.

"Supposedly."

"By who?"

Calvin shrugged. "I don't know. A cowboy?"

I took the journal and tossed it to the bed. "Speaking of, let's go to the saloon, get some trade whiskey, ask a cowboy if he needs a ride…."

Calvin rolled his eyes and slung an arm over my shoulders. "Bringing you here was a huge mistake."

"Wanna watch me unload my six-shooter?"

Calvin shoved me into the hallway. "Keep it up."

"Hang on—just one more."

"See what happens."

"But we can save a horse if we—"

Calvin shut the door.

A beat.

Then he opened it. "Put your phone in the room."

"What if Max calls?"

"The Emporium is already closed."

"What if I need to know the time?"

"I'm wearing a watch."

"I have to read your wrist if I want to know the time?"

"Yes. Go—or no gunpowder whiskey for you."

"Christ, Cal." I shoved the door open, went to the nightstand, and set my phone beside the alarm clock. I noticed the suitcase was near the armoire and bathroom doorway when I turned, and I hesitated a moment. Hadn't Calvin put that against the wall?

"Come on, Sheriff."

I blinked, shook my head, and stepped into the hall. "Did you know bartenders in the Wild West would cut whiskey with water, cayenne, and actual gunpowder? One of the nicknames for the drink was coffin varnish."

"Welcome to the Diamond Belle, gentlemen." A bartender in—well, not historically accurate, but the effort was appreciated nonetheless—attire, set his hands on the counter. He was middle-aged, fit, and sported an actual handlebar mustache. His nametag said Mick. "What can I get you both?"

Calvin inquired after trade whiskey, and the bartender said they did, in fact, offer it.

Mick placed two tumblers before us, the contents a bit cloudy-looking. "It's more for the novelty than the flavor."

I picked up my glass, tapped it against Calvin's, then took a sip. "There's actual cayenne in this?" I asked, pursing my lips a little at the lingering heat.

Mick nodded. "And did you pick up the metallic note?"

"Uh-huh."

"That's the gunpowder."

"What doesn't kill you," Calvin said, taking a second sip.

Mick gave a hearty laugh. "That's the spirit. Where you gents from?"

"New York," I answered.

"Oh, yeah? The state or the city?"

"City," I clarified.

"And what brings you out to humble Durango?"

"I was told we needed a vacation."

"He tries very hard to make it sound like a punishment," Calvin added, a wry smile on his face as he rubbed my back a few times.

Mick smoothed his mustache and said, "You picked a damn good destination, if you don't mind my saying. I visited twenty-two years ago and forgot to ever leave." He jutted a thumb over his shoulder in indication while asking, "You gents booked at the Strater?"

Calvin agreed.

"Great place. Great place. Watch out for ghosts." He added that last comment as an almost afterthought.

"I'll look both ways before crossing the street," I agreed.

Mick stroked his 'stache again. "What floor you on—at the Strater?"

"Third," I said. "Why?"

"Folks usually hear things up there. Feel things."

I glanced at Calvin, who shrugged and sipped his gunpowder concoction. I looked at Mick again. "*Things*."

"Creaking at night, like someone's walking around."

"It is a hotel. People come and go at all hours," I said.

"Sure."

"And it's quite old—over 130 years. It's bound to have a squeaky floorboard or two."

"Yup."

"But?" I pressed.

"Guests report the steps originating from *inside* their room," Mick concluded.

I didn't usually get drunk.

Tipsy, sure. But he-will-have-regrets-tomorrow drunk? Let's just say it'd been a long time since I was a dumbass college freshman. So the very small, still rational part of my brain that hadn't been drowned in distilled malt was experiencing some secondhand embarrassment on my behalf while I all but manhandled Calvin outside our hotel room.

"It must be the altitude," I whispered as I gathered Calvin's T-shirt in both hands from behind and yanked it up enough that I could touch the hard planes of his stomach.

He put an arm across his front to stop my hands as he dug the key card from his pocket. "I think that's a myth."

"Altitude is very real."

He stifled a laugh. "Jesus, you are drunk."

"I'll say. Mick fucked me up nice and good. Did you tip him?" As soon as I heard a *click* and the turn of the handle, I pushed Calvin forward so he stumbled against the door. I pulled my hands from his warm body, turned him, grabbed his face, and kissed Calvin hard.

Calvin took my hips and yanked me flush against himself. His mouth left mine, found my wrist, kissed it, then nudged my hand out of the way so he could kiss my neck.

"I think I'm drunk enough for dirty talk," I murmured.

Calvin groaned like a man coming unglued. "Fuck." He shoved back from the still-open door, let it fall shut, flipped the light switch, then killed the mood by saying, "What the hell?"

"What?" I adjusted my glasses and turned. Our suitcase lay on the floor, open, with the clothes askew, as if someone had recently rifled through the contents.

Calvin's cop-mode activated immediately, and he used one hand to guide me to stand behind him. He checked under the bed before flipping on the bathroom light and stepping inside. Calvin looked behind the door, behind the shower curtain, and then he reappeared, frowning. "This would be incredibly stupid of a housekeeper. They're assigned rooms. They're assigned section keys for entering."

I crouched and pawed through the clothing. "Nothing's missing."

"Not the point."

I leaned back on my heels and stared up at Calvin. "Can it be the point for, like, thirty minutes?"

"We need to deal with this."

"Twenty minutes."

"Sebastian. Get a drink of water. I'm calling the front desk."

I sighed and stood. "Bummer."

Blondie, the winker who'd checked us in, was standing in our room by the time I'd taken a seat on the edge of the mattress with a plastic cup of lukewarm water. I sipped and watched the back-and-forth between him and Calvin, who—always polite—was still very commanding in these sorts of situations.

"I'm *so* sorry," Blondie said for maybe the fourth time. "Nothing like this has ever happened at the Strater before. There must be a logical—ah, Helga!" he said when a short woman, her dark hair tied back in a ponytail, poked her head inside. "Helga's our only member of housekeeping on the clock this late in the evening," he explained to Calvin before turning to the woman. "Thank you for rushing up here. Tell me, do you know who was assigned this room for check-in prep?"

Helga seemed confused and said, "I was. I did three rooms on this floor. This was the last."

"You never returned after check-in?" Blondie inquired.

Helga peered around the corner at me, took in the bulky antique furnishings, then shook her head. "No, of course not. I helped Marcy with that premium queen-queen afterward—

the one those honeymooners trashed? It took us hours. Then I went on break, and I was in the middle of laundry when you called."

Calvin nodded as he followed her story. He put his hands in his pockets and asked calmly, "You still have your card to access your section of rooms?"

Helga produced the card in question.

"It was never out of your hands?" Calvin continued.

"No, never." She finally asked, "What's happened?"

"It would appear that someone entered the room while our guests were at dinner," Blondie explained as he pointed to the still-open suitcase.

"Oh my God," Helga said, now realizing the gravity of the questions being asked of her. "It wasn't me. No way."

"It's all right," Calvin said, holding a hand up. "Don't worry—I believe you."

Helga's shoulders dropped a little as she let out a breath. "It could have been the ghost…."

I leaned back on the mattress to grab the ghost diary I'd tossed there earlier. "Good point. Let's see if anyone in the past reported a disembodied spirit with a penchant for boxer briefs."

Calvin sighed at that and thanked both Helga and Blondie—the latter offering us a different room, which Calvin declined, comped breakfast for the rest of our visit, which Calvin reluctantly accepted at Blondie's unrelenting insistence, then promised further investigation into the matter before wishing us a good night.

Calvin shut and locked the door. He glanced at me.

"Delayed sexual gratification is not a kink I'm into," I stated. I put the half-empty cup on the nightstand. "Can I have my way with you now or what?"

"You're really not concerned, are you?"

"I'm concerned my blue balls might have lasting health consequences." I tossed the ghost diary aside again. "Now please get naked so I can fuck you. Before my liquid courage is metabolized."

I awoke with a start but wasn't sure why. Calvin had one leg between mine, his head on my chest, his arm wrapped around my waist. His breathing sounded even and low—sex-coma sleep. I thought he must have shifted and that's what woke me, but I had the strangest impression that the sense of touch hadn't been responsible.

It was something I heard.

A rustle of—clothing, maybe.

Which made no sense, because we were both naked under the blankets.

I cracked open one eye and took in the room. Greatly out-of-focus it might have been without glasses, but the only functioning cells in my eyes—rods—performed specifically in low-light situations, so I was able to pretty quickly take in the outline of the windows, the low shape of the dresser and attached mirror, the massive armoire with its open door—

The hell?

Then a deadbolt turned, its quiet click like an avalanche in the Swiss Alps to my hyper-attuned hearing. I jerked my head on the pillow and watched the front door silently swing open and a whitish shape drift into the hallway. The door was carefully closed behind the… *thing.*

I thought of Mick and his mustache. *"Folks usually hear things up there."*

A ghost?

No.

I was still a little drunk, could feel the disorientation as I pushed Calvin off and sat up, but I was not stupid enough to think a long-dead housekeeper from the turn of the century was just checking in at midnight to see if we needed mints on the pillows. Plus, what sort of ghost had to unlock a door to leave? Wasn't the whole spooky aspect the fact that they could walk through walls and shit?

I struggled free from the blankets and clumsily got to my feet. Calvin didn't wake, which was surprising, but I guess a cross-country flight, seven-hour drive, liquor, and some… um… amazing hotel sex was what it took to knock him out for the better part of the night. I took a step forward, got tangled in Calvin's jeans on the floor, and nearly face-planted.

"Dammit," I hissed. I'd somehow managed to slide my foot right into the back pocket—wait a minute. I crouched, thoroughly checked, but no… Calvin's wallet was gone. And considering how'd I'd been groping him, let me just assure that it'd been there when he was being undressed.

That spectral thing hadn't been a ghost. I mean, *duh*. It'd been an intruder. And the rustling sound I'd heard was this motherfucker stealing Calvin's cash, credit card, license—*hell*, he kept his shield in that wallet when he was off duty. I sobered considerably as I grabbed my glasses off the nightstand, found my underwear, and yanked them on before checking the door's peephole. The benefit to always forgetting to remove my red-tinted contacts was that I wasn't immediately blinded by the light from the third-floor hallway.

I didn't see anyone, so I yanked open the door and ran out. I belatedly realized, with the exception of my boxer briefs, I was very naked. I reached the banister around the stairwell in the middle of the layout, set my hands on the worn and polished wood, then leaned over. It didn't appear there was anyone attempting The Great Escape via this route. I looked to the right—dead-end nook with some closed doors, mirroring the same setup on my left, where our room was. I tiptoed backward a few steps to look down the long hallway opposite of Main Avenue.

And there he—she—er—Wannabe Casper was, wearing a long, shapeless, white or maybe gray dress. Something akin to the cheap, mass-produced "historical" attires the staff in the saloon wore, except this was a matronly ensemble and not a sexy bar girl. Casper was standing in front of another guest room, seeming to be struggling with their key card.

"Hey!" I shouted, my voice too loud in the still and silent hotel.

Casper jumped and spun toward me. I was too far to make out any serious details, but I was fairly certain Casper was a man, dressed as a woman, with Halloween face paint on for a *dead* effect. He panicked, a combination of having been caught and having been caught by a man just *this side* of naked. Casper bolted down the hall, then seemed to rethink that plan, and reversed course for the stairwell.

I raced forward to cut him off, but Casper dodged and ran around the far side of the banister to put distance between us. He was seconds away from the stairs, and then there'd be no way I could catch him without taking a tumble and breaking my neck. We'd spend the rest of this amazing vacation calling banks to freeze cards, scheduling an appointment for a driver's license replacement, and worse than having to deal with the DMV, Calvin would have to report his badge being stolen.

In a split-second decision, I picked up a potted fern from a stand beside a mirror and framed painting on the wall to my right, took aim as Casper rounded the corner, then chucked it.

I was standing on the landing of the second floor, surrounded by soil, broken pottery, and one fern that didn't look like it'd survive the assault. I still had no shoes or pants, but at least I'd been given one of my sweaters, so I had that on with my arms firmly crossed over my chest. An EMT was shining a penlight into Casper's eyes, checking for a potential concussion caused by either the pot or the fall down the stairs, while a uniformed officer was stooped and securing handcuffs on Casper from behind. Calvin stood about a foot away, talking to a second officer. He wore only his jeans, which were low-hanging and snug on his hips. He'd come rushing out of our room after I'd woken the entire third floor, and probably a few actual resting spirits, by braining Casper in the head with a fucking houseplant.

The third-floor guests were watching us over the banister. Blondie was on the landing with us, alternating between panic, profound confusion, and one or two distracted, lingering glances at my bare legs.

"I didn't have time to get dressed," I said, very matter-of-factly.

Blondie stuttered a little. "Y-yes, sir. It's—it's understandable." He turned his attention toward Casper. "You're fired, Sheldon."

Sheldon blinked his eyes a few times when the penlight was removed. "Yeah, I figured," he grumbled.

The cop, his hands on his belt and looking very butch, asked in a bellowing voice, "Mr. Goodwin, when did you get yourself a copy of the housekeeping key cards?"

"Few weeks ago," Sheldon muttered, mostly to the floor.

"And you've been pilfering valuables from guests?" Butch concluded, putting two and two together and looking very pleased with his investigative skills.

Sheldon nodded and added, "I was using 321 to store my costume and goods."

"That's where you were going when I caught you?" I asked.

Sheldon nodded.

"What happened?" Blondie interjected.

Sheldon shrugged, the motion limited by his cuffed hands at his back. "I guess the card got demagnetized. I couldn't get inside, and then this psycho threw a fern at my head."

"You stole my boyfriend's wallet," I snapped. "Give it back, by the way."

Butch leaned over Sheldon and patted down his fake boobs before finding a pouch sewn into the chest of the dress. He removed Calvin's wallet and passed it to me. "Is this it?"

I opened it and was confirming the contents when Calvin joined me, patting his back pockets as he stared at the wallet. "This is yours," I said, handing it to him.

Calvin raised a light-colored brow. "Want to fill me in, baby?"

"Something woke me up, and I noticed the armoire—" I felt my face grow hot, and I spun toward Sheldon again. "You were in our room all night?"

He had the decency to look chagrined. "I was in there— in the armoire—when you checked in. I didn't even have time to open the suitcase before you'd come back to drop your phone off. I don't bother taking phones—too easy to get caught, what with GPS. But you didn't have shit on you. Hours later, I realized I'd dropped my key card to 321, so I went to check your room for it, then you both came back… so… I hid."

"I said a lot of things under the influence of alcohol," I murmured.

"Yeah, you definitely did," Sheldon agreed.

Calvin cleared his throat. "Why the getup?"

Sheldon tried to shrug again. "Ghost stories keep the tourists coming. Anything moved or missing is blamed on the ghost. And if I *were* seen… they think I'm a ghost." He narrowed his eyes at me. "Except you."

"Well, I'm not an idiot," I supplied.

Boisterous Butch said to Calvin, "You don't seem particularly surprised by this incident, Detective. I guess you see all kinds of crazy shit in New York, don't you?"

Calvin cast a sideways look at me.

"All in a day's work," I told him.

INTERPERSONAL RELATIONSHIP STUDIES ON THE WAY TO THE COFFEE HOUSE

—

Before *The Mystery of the Bones*
POV: Calvin Winter

—

Quinn stuck the end of a cigarillo between her lips as we stepped out of the precinct. She fished a lighter from her suit pocket, struck the spark wheel once, twice, and brought a flame to the tip on the third try. "Starbucks?" she asked on the exhale, and vanilla-scented smoke briefly mingled with the bite of November air.

"Sure."

"I'll have a cold brew."

"You're implying it's on me."

Quinn took another drag. "Why would I imply? It's your turn."

"I bought on Monday."

"And I bet you this morning that the GSR results for the Park case would come back negative."

I raised an eyebrow and said, "I wasn't aware there was a cost to losing that bet."

"There's always a cost," she said, pointing the cigarillo at me.

The top of Quinn's head barely met my shoulders, and I could easily bench press two of her, but her authority and self-assurance were larger than life. She was a bit of a smart aleck in her own regard and had a zero-bullshit policy that could rub some folks the wrong way. But it was those quirks about Quinn that allowed her to challenge me every day, both as a detective and as a man, and I loved her dearly for the constant push. In September, we'd celebrated our first full year as partners working homicide. We'd gone out for drinks, and I'd given her a repurposed Victorian holiday card (Sebastian assisted, if it wasn't obvious) of a frog murdered with a dagger and a thief frog absconding with a bag of money. Sebastian had tried to explain why this bizarre imagery was once a Christmas card, but he'd gone off the rails and ended up on a long-winded rant about Victorian print jokes that he felt were still quite funny and relevant to modern times.

I hadn't bothered to interrupt him.

My relationship with Quinn was something special, though. After the Curiosities case, Sebastian had been very vocal and adamant about making changes to my routine for mental health purposes, but Quinn had been… *quiet* wasn't the right description…. She'd been supportive of the changes without acknowledging why they were being implemented.

At the time, I could hardly speak to Sebastian about… *everything*. But her frankness—*Let's take a walk, my ass is falling asleep. I need some coffee and nicotine. Go call your nutcase boyfriend.* All these minute alterations for my benefit were done without ever vocalizing her concern for my well-being. And maybe it'd been selfish of me, but I'd appreciated her refusal to say there was anything deeper but the statement on the surface. Because at the time, Sebastian's concern had been crippling, and I don't think I'd have been able to shoulder anxiety from both of them.

Sometimes concern felt like guilt, if that made any sense.

And I knew she and Sebastian talked about and enforced those changes together, but I'd learned that what works for me was my best friend simply being there and not having to say what we both already knew. Anyway… I'd done my best to express my appreciation for her in that silly card, and when she'd gotten very quiet after reading the inscription, I'd asked if she was going to cry. Quinn immediately dead-legged me and then told the bartender I was treating her to the top shelf that night.

I raised my fist for a quick game of Rock, Paper, Scissors.

Quinn stuck the cigarillo between her lips and raised one in return.

We counted to three—I threw scissors and her, rock.

Quinn knocked her hand against mine and then called loud enough that a few uniformed cops mingling by the doors turned to look at us, "When *will* he learn that I am the reigning champ?"

"Is this really what you're going to write home about, Quinn?" I asked, tucking my hands into my coat pockets.

"I want a venti."

"You can't drink an entire venti."

"Half is for later," she explained. "And you know what? While you're at it, grab me one of those double chocolate brownies."

"I never agreed to food."

"Best two out of three," Quinn answered, holding up her fist again.

"All right, all right. And a brownie, you hedonist. I'll be right back."

I walked to the end of the block, where a Starbucks had smartly cashed in on some real estate that'd become available during the summer. If there were two professions that could single-handedly keep the coffee industry afloat, it was filmmakers and cops—and this wasn't a TV neighborhood.

I pulled the door open and a *whoosh* of central heat greeted me. The scent of ground coffee beans and warmed paninis hung heavy in the air. A year ago, I probably wouldn't have recognized the smoky female voice singing on the shop speakers, but Sebastian was such an enthusiast of jazz, blues, and the early years of R&B that I could now place Etta James almost immediately. "Something's Got a Hold on Me," which Sebastian sang around the apartment on a fairly routine basis.

"Hi, Calvin," called Camille, the always perky barista, waving enthusiastically from behind one of the two registers.

"Camille," I said in greeting. I placed Quinn's order, and when she asked if I wanted my usual latte, I opted instead for a house brew. To be honest, it wasn't much of a step up from the hours-old precinct coffee that could have doubled for car oil, but despite his insatiable sweet tooth, my ornery curmudgeon preferred his coffee dark and bitter, and Etta had dropped Sebastian to the forefront of my thoughts.

I paid, moved to the pickup counter, and took my phone out. I pulled up the last text conversation I'd had with Sebastian yesterday: *Fred Astaire cuute?*

That question had stemmed from a thirty-minute argument between him and Max, which had ended in a stalemate, of which I was then requested to break. Now, if

Sebastian had asked me whether I thought Humphrey Bogart or James Stewart was attractive—yes, absolutely—but not Astaire. However, since I knew where Sebastian stood on this particular subject, and because I hadn't wanted to sleep on the couch last night, I'd agreed. From the flurry of texts I received afterward from Max, Sebastian had preened for the rest of the afternoon and Max insisted it was unfair to have me, the fiancé, break the tie.

A typical day when you're in love with Sebastian Snow.

My thumb hovered over the keyboard as I considered a message. I didn't have anything special to say, and simply considered sending a quick: *Hey, baby, just thinking of you.* I could practically hear Sebastian's response to that, in his deep, dry voice that was always a touch sardonic.

He'd try to hold back a smile, but he loves when I call him *baby*, so that fight wouldn't last long. And he'd say something to the effect of "I'm clearly the deadweight in this relationship." Then, because Sebastian was always on, always thinking, always trying to figure something out, to such an extent that he could be utterly unaware of what was going on around him at times, the conversation would pull a one-eighty and we'd be discussing the finer points of the Singer sewing machine for the next twenty minutes.

Point A to Point Q.

I settled on the text, *What're you working on right now?*

"Winter?"

I locked my phone and looked up. CSU detective and Sebastian's ex, Neil Millett, was tucking his wallet into his back pocket. "Millett," I said cordially. "What brings you down this way?"

"A scene a few blocks from here." He reluctantly approached the pickup counter, slid his hands into his trouser pockets, and asked, "How're you?" Millett had never been one for small talk, so his stiff attempt, whether authentic or more likely because he didn't want to pretend he hadn't seen me for however many minutes he waited for his coffee, caught me by surprise.

"I'm okay," I answered. "How about yourself?"

Millett's gaze wandered, lingered on the barista steaming milk for an order. "Living," he eventually said, and the honesty of his reply, the emotional gravity of that single word—I understood it all too well.

Living and being alive were two very different states of existence.

"So you're engaged." Millett colored a little before adding, more gently, "Sebastian texted me last week."

I nodded. "Yeah."

"He tried to tell me about a maroon tree or something," Millett continued, "but he kept typing *moron*, which I kept pointing out, and then he got frustrated and all-caps told me to fuck off."

I shook my head and said around a growing smile, "That sounds about right."

Millett looked at the barista again. "I don't know why he won't use voice-to-text."

"He doesn't trust it."

Millett snorted. "He's such an asshole."

"Sometimes," I said with a chuckle.

"I won't tell him you said that." Millett collected his cup when the barista called out *Neil!* and slapped it down on the countertop. He stared at the spelling of his name for a moment, frowned, then started to turn toward the door without another word.

"Neil?" I echoed.

Millett stumbled a step, looked at me, and raised a skeptical eyebrow.

"I never properly thanked you."

"For what?" he asked cautiously.

"For… being there for Sebastian. I don't mean when he was in the hospital over the summer. He's been happy, having you as a friend again."

Millett frowned and cast his dark eyes to his expensive shoes. He looked like he wanted to be absolutely anywhere but here. But after a minute—and it was a minute—he raised his head and said, "You and I aren't always going to agree or see eye-to-eye. But you're part of the package now, so we'll both do our best."

I nodded again.

"And please don't do something stupid like invite me over for dinner."

"I won't."

Millett gripped his cup so tight, the lid looked about ready to pop off. "I love Sebastian. He's my only friend." He held his hand out, shook mine, and said thickly, "Congratulations."

"Thank you."

Millett left it at that, turned, and walked out the door.

"Sorry for that wait on the cold brew, Calvin," Camille said suddenly, bursting the little bubble that had seemed to envelop me.

"Oh. No problem," I said. I flashed her a quick, automatic smile and was tucking my phone away in order to carry both coffees and the brownie when it buzzed in my hand.

Sebastian Snow.

I opened the text to see that he'd answered my question.

Nothing. Just thinking of you.

SOMEONE'S IN THE WALL

—

Before The Mystery of the Bones
POV: Sebastian Snow—

I sat at the table-for-two in the front room, wearing nothing but a pair of boxer briefs and a T-shirt, eating Lucky Charms and scowling at my phone's screen. "I'm cold," I stated when Calvin entered from the kitchen.

"Probably because it's November and you're in your skivvies."

I looked up. "Do you recall the circumstances of our meeting?"

Calvin set his thermos on the table. "I woke up one day and you were in my bed," he answered, knotting the tie around his neck. "Thought it was a bit strange, but you were cute, so I let it slide."

"I'm serious."

"Well, what kind of question is that, baby?"

"I think there's someone in the wall."

Calvin said nothing as he adjusted his shoulder holster, picked up his suit coat from the back of the chair opposite me, and pulled it on. He then walked to the coatrack beside the door, collected his winter jacket, and returned to kiss me goodbye. "I'm going to go to work now."

"*Calvin.*"

"There's nothing in the walls, Sebastian."

"I heard it last night—behind the bed. It woke me up."

"It was probably a rat."

"It was way bigger—"

"Call the super today and have him schedule an exterminator." Calvin kissed me again. "Have a good day."

"If it turns out that Fortunato is dead in our walls, I will never stop saying *I told you so*," I called after him.

Calvin opened the front door, looked over his shoulder, and said, "If one of our neighbors pulls a *Tell-Tale Heart*—"

"*Cask of Amontillado.*"

"—I'll let you spank me."

My eyebrows crept to my hairline. "I don't need a reason to spank you."

Calvin shut the door.

I glanced at Dillon, who cocked his head to one side. "Well, I *don't*," I reiterated before standing and collecting the bowl of soggy cereal. "I just prefer the action in reverse. Why am I saying this to a dog."

I left the bowl in the kitchen sink, went upstairs, and got dressed for a day of errands and chores that absolutely did *not* involve a mysterious thing in the wall. I tugged my arms through a long-sleeved thermal, pulled it over my head, and put on a clean pair of jeans. I went to the nightstand, grabbed my wallet and keys, then put a knee on the mattress and leaned over the headboard. I couldn't see any sort of hole or break in the drywall that'd suggest something had been trying to escape last night. Even though it *had* been loud enough to be a human trying to dig their way out with a spoon, and it wasn't my fault that, for the first night in a week, Calvin had managed to sleep deeper than the dead the one time I'd have preferred he easily woke, thank you very much.

I pressed my ear against the wall and listened. At first there was nothing but that strange, fishbowl hum that seemed to exist in the bit of space between Neighbor A and Neighbor B in a densely populated urban environment—but then I heard it. A shifting or scratching that was just *too fucking big* to be a rat. I leaned back and pounded once on the wall.

Silence.

Calvin might have thought I was being ridiculous, but our loft mirrored 4A across the hall. Maybe he'd heard *the thing* last night. We'd only been tenants for six months, but 4A had lived here for years, as far as I could tell. He'd be acquainted with any potential animal, man, ghost, or curse roaming between the walls.

I hurried to the closet, slipped on my loafers, grabbed the basket of dirty laundry, and went downstairs. I snatched my phone from the table on my way out the door, and once in the hall, knocked on 4A.

The chain lock made a *shiiick* as it was undone, a deadbolt turned, and 4A poked his head out. "Oh. Locked out again?"

You come home one time without your phone, keys, or shoes, and your neighbor never lets you live it down....

I held the basket against my hip and raised the keys in my other hand. "No, I'm good. I just had a question."

"I need to get ready for work."

"It'll be quick."

He sighed a bit melodramatically and leaned against the doorjamb.

"Have you heard any strange sounds in our shared wall, up in the loft?"

"Like your headboard two nights ago?"

I felt my face immediately warm. "Er—"

4A raised both hands and smacked the back of one against his other palm, emulating the rhythmic beat of me having my brains fucked out of my skull on Saturday night.

"We pulled the bed away from the wall."

4A frowned and lowered his hands.

"And I slipped that apology note under your door the next morning. What do you want from me?"

"Goodbye." He shut the door.

So much for that angle of investigation.

I made my way down to the basement. I found someone else's wet clothes that'd been left in the wash overnight, rolled my eyes, and tossed the garments onto the long table against the far wall—a nice, passive-aggressive way of saying "fuck you, this is a shared space." I spent another minute holding my phone toward the ceiling, moving in small circles, searching for a signal strong enough to pay for the load, then hiked back to the apartment.

The building was quiet—no heat clanking through the piping, and most residents seemed to have already left for work. I reached the fourth-floor landing and slowed as I moved down the hall. I put a hand on the wall outside our apartment and pressed my ear against it.

"The cough's a mere nothing," I quoted Fortunato. "It will not kill me. I shall not die from a cough." And when Montresor would have uttered his knowing and chilling, "True—true," there was a loud scramble on the other side of the drywall. I yelped, jumped backward, and pointed an accusing finger at the wall. "How'd you get down here from the loft?" I protested.

It took a moment for me to remember I was standing in the hallway, shouting at the wall like an actual insane person. I shook myself, retrieved my keys, and went inside. Dillon was standing near the table where I'd been munching cereal, head cocked, staring just to the right.

"You heard it too?" I shut the door. "No one else does." I tossed the laundry basket to the floor. "What the fuck is it?"

Dillon turned his head to the other side, as if weighing an answer he was unwilling to share.

"A lot of help you are," I grumbled.

My phone vibrated in my pocket, and I half expected a psychic text from Calvin to tell me to call the damn super and stop trying to convince myself a person was stuck in the wall, but it was instead a notification from our bank. I brought the screen close and read: *Suspicious Activity—did you approve a transaction from account ending x5555 for $902.37? Reply YES or NO.*

"Holy shit." I tapped *NO* and sent the text. An immediate response came that the card associated with the account had been closed for fraud protection and to call my bank immediately. I groaned, dialed customer support, and was eventually routed through the automatic system to a living human.

The situation immediately went downhill.

"You didn't attempt a transaction for nine hundred and two dollars and thirty-seven cents at Apple?" the woman asked me.

"No, absolutely not. I don't even know how this card number was stolen. It's a joint account my fiancé and I use to pay bills."

"Er—I don't see her name on this account."

"He," I corrected. "Calvin Winter."

"Oh."

"Can you just flag that transaction? I won't even buy myself a computer for that price, let alone a complete stranger."

"Yes, sir, I've done that, but it can take up to thirty days to be investigated."

I pinched the bridge of my nose and said dryly, "Awesome. Whatever. Can you reissue new cards in the meantime?"

"Well, I'll need to talk to the primary name on the account."

"Isn't that what we're doing right now?"

"That'd be Mr. Winter—it looks like he opened the account."

"All right, but it's joint. You do see my name, don't you?"

"Yes, sir."

"And Mr. Winter is my fiancé, so—"

"Unfortunately, I'm only legally allowed to reissue cards to the primary name, since you're not listed as a married couple on the account."

I laughed, but it wasn't out of humor. "You're joking, right?"

"No, sir."

"Ma'am, we live at the same address. We both drop money into this account. I'm literally holding the card associated with it in my hand. I can tell you Mr. Winter's social. His blood type. Shoe size."

"For security purposes—"

"Oh my God. Fine. I'll call my fiancé at work and tell him he needs to stop being a detective and instead has to fix our locked account because the bank refuses to acknowledge my name."

"Thank you for calling—"

"No." I hung up and saw two texts from Calvin waiting to be read.

What's this fraud notice on our joint account?

Did you call the bank?

I growled and angrily texted back: *Yes bt when I said I was ur fiance teh rep refusedd me access.*

Three dots populated on the screen as Calvin typed—he must have been watching his phone. *Are you serious?*

As if Id jok.

I'll call.

Sry.

It's not your fault.

Yuu gong to rip them a new ass?

Yes.

I admit that I laughed at Calvin's very frank text, because I could already envision how that conversation would go. He'd be nothing but calm and polite—polar opposite of my grouchiness and nonexistent patience—but he'd still manage to somehow put the fear of God into someone. I was jealous of Calvin's ability to wrangle people with just a calculated look or carefully constructed statement. He was always able to commandeer total respect simply by walking into a room, and meanwhile Phone Rep Gertrude from Tennessee fed me a total line of homophobic bullshit I couldn't wriggle around no matter what I tried. Such was life, I guessed.

I ran to Duane Reade while the wash finished its cycle, Calvin handled the bank, and the not-person in the wall kept living their best life. We'd pretty much run out of all household necessities at once, and Calvin had wandered around the apartment last night, writing a list. He's not typically a listmaker, so I knew it was serious and that my future would be nothing but a significant other's unrelenting disappointment if I didn't go shopping—especially since Calvin had to deal with Gertrude now.

The sky was spitting big fat snowflakes. Not enough to stick, but it was definitely a threat that winter was knocking down autumn's door. The overcast morning was easy on the eyes, at least, until I reached the end of the block and the entire street was gridlocked by strobing firetrucks. I squinted while moving around a growing crowd to see—

"Good God," I muttered.

A firefighter broke the outer glass wall of my neighborhood Duane Reade and black smoke billowed out. A few men barreled into the building after him.

"Fuck this fucking fuck of a Monday!" a woman wearing a pharmacist's coat shouted. "Dammit, Dave."

"It wasn't me!" a man—Dave, I had to presume—whined.

She smacked his shoulder hard enough that he recoiled. "You put your Egg McMuffin in the microwave again, didn't you?"

"It was cold by the time I got to work."

"You have to take the wrapper off," she cried. "We tell you every fucking day, Dave! *No wrappers!*"

I made a careful retreat and walked a few blocks uptown to a CVS. I grabbed a hand basket at the front doors and began perusing the aisles. It was a shame about Dave, because that Duane Reade had been *my store*.

Let me explain. There were nearly nine million of us living in this city, and the average New Yorker walked anywhere between two and five miles a day simply to and from work. When calculating in the necessity of errands, there's suddenly a benefit to having a drugstore and Starbucks on every block. And once you found *that* store—distance and stock taken into account—it became yours. You were suddenly a points-using member. You knew where every single item was. You knew which employee to get at checkout who wouldn't give you a hard time. It was *your* store.

And Dave had set my store on fire.

So it took twice as long to find what I needed at this not-my-store, only to realize they were out of stock on paper towels, dish soap, and Calvin's preferred brand of razor. I spent ten minutes comparing available alternatives, trying to decide on a replacement. I didn't use manual razors, so what the hell did I know. If I went cheap, I'd undoubtedly be the cause of a cut-up face. If I went expensive, I was probably paying for marketing. Ultimately, I chose the expensive route. It seemed safer.

I dug the list out of my pocket. *Got that, out of stock, out of stock, got that, got—no, wait.* I left the personal grooming and wandered into the next aisle—sexual wellness. When Calvin had given me the requests last night, I'd pointed out that I seemed to buy condoms or lube more than I did candy, which I felt said something.

Calvin had slid his hands into his pockets and said, looking down at me where I sat on the couch with my laptop, "Are you complaining?"

"Making an observation."

"We can tone it down."

"Okay, but, hang on—"

"Just blowjobs."

I'd made a face and asked, "To clarify, you're threatening me with blowjobs, correct?"

"If you stopped buying the little bottles," Calvin continued, "lube wouldn't be a weekly purchase, like eggs and coffee creamer."

"Let me head out to Costco and buy a bucket of lube."

"With an industrial pump," Calvin agreed.

I'd narrowed my eyes and studied his flat expression. "I can't tell if you're joking."

Calvin leaned down, wrapped a big hand around my throat, and gave a little squeeze. "Buy another two-ounce bottle again and I promise you'll find out."

"My ass is still recovering from last night."

"Mine's just fine." Calvin straightened, and walking toward the kitchen, had called over his shoulder, "And if we weren't out of lube, I could have had a deep-dicking tonight."

I shook myself, shoved the paper into my coat pocket, and walked midway down the aisle to what was an almost-empty shelf. "Oh, come on," I whispered. I bent down to read the remaining labels.

Wet and Juicy Watermelon-Flavored Lube.

Fertility Buddy! Provides Antioxidant Support to Sperm.

Female Stimulation Serum—Not a Personal Lubricant.

Jesus Christ.

Well, considering one wasn't even a lube, I wasn't looking to get pregnant, and most importantly, absolutely neither of us were going to smell like a fucking fruit cocktail, I left the store with a mostly unfulfilled list.

While walking back to our building, I opened my texts, chose the one person in my contacts list who, to be honest, would probably answer me truthfully, and sent a message to my buddy Aubrey Grant: *If smeone suggst room-temp buttter fr lube what would you say.*

That's when I realized I'd tapped Neil, whose name was one above Aubrey's in the list of recent text conversations.

I quickly sent: *Sry wrong person.*

I received a reply before I could even close out of his name: *Never text me again.*

Geez. What a grouch.

After sending the question to the correct recipient, I pocketed my cell, unlocked the front door of our building, and slipped inside. The laundry was definitely done at this point, so I made a quick detour to the basement. Asshole's wet clothes were still on the table. I set my CVS bag aside, opened the front-loading washer, and an entire drum of dirty, soapy, freezing cold water gushed out, soaking my pants, shoes—going absolutely *everywhere*.

I stood there for a moment, hand still on the door, staring at the sopping wet clothes hanging out of the washer and then down at my nice shoes. Yes, they were loafers, but they were, like, a classy loafer, and now they were full of dirty Tide water. Calmly, I bent down and took the handles of my paper bag, because I was going to consider this a lost cause, run away, and maybe live out the remainder of my life in the wilds of Central Park. But as I lifted the bag, its soaked bottom tore and everything I'd bought dropped to the floor.

I'd put in a call to the super and left him in the basement to fix the shitshow that'd just transpired. I carried my purchases upstairs, *shlop, shlop, shlopp*ing up all four flights, and let myself into the apartment. After kicking the door shut, I heard it.

A screech from inside the wall, like a dying old woman.

I dropped my shit, spun on one heel, and stared at the wall Dillon and I had both heard the rustling in earlier.

"Hello?" I called loudly.

She screeched again, even louder.

"No one in the wall *my ass*," I snapped, throwing the apartment door open once more and storming into the hall. My phone buzzed in my pocket as I marched back down to the basement. The super had a maintenance room off the laundry, and after a Monday of 4A, Gertrude, Dave, and whoever the hell else was at fault for driving me to drink before noon, I was going to handle this Someone in the Wall situation myself. "*What?*" I snapped upon answering my phone.

"Oh my God," Aubrey said. "You didn't use the butter already, did you?"

"Butter?"

"Never text me sex questions. Those are important. You call me, Sebastian. You need to go clean your ass right now."

"I didn't use butter. I'm not even having sex," I said, making my way back down the creaking basement staircase.

"Thank goodness," Aubrey mumbled. "Because it's dairy, you know? And it can go rancid, and then you've got a bacterial infection in your—"

"Please stop."

"If you're looking to get kinky in the bedroom—"

"I don't want to get kinky," I replied, opening the maintenance room door and flipping the light switch.

"You need to ask an expert. I love you, Seb, but you're too vanilla. Your X-rays would end up on BuzzFeed and the entire internet would be laughing about whatever you stuck up your butt."

"I'm not vanilla. And you need to lay off my butt."

"I bet you only have sex with the lights off, below the covers."

"I don't." I found what I needed propped against a worktable and grabbed the handle of a ten-pound sledgehammer. "Just because you have a—what's the dick piercing called?"

"Prince Albert."

"Just because you have a Prince Albert—"

"I don't have a Prince Albert," Aubrey interrupted. "Ears, nose, nipples, and belly, darling."

I grunted while smacking the light switch with my elbow and walking out.

Super glanced from the open doorway of the laundry room as I passed. "You break it?" he called.

"I didn't break it," I answered over my shoulder.

"I find many socks under the wash plate!"

I paused halfway up the stairs and turned to Super. "What color are the socks?"

"Are you asking me?" Aubrey asked in my ear.

Super held up two handfuls of soaking-wet socks. "Many colors."

"I don't own many colors. Mostly black. I had a red pair, but those were a mistake."

Super shook the socks in my direction. "Maybe they are Boyfriend's socks."

"Boyfriend doesn't wear colorful socks."

"Who the hell are you talking to, Seb?" Aubrey tried again.

"My super," I answered.

Said man dropped the socks to the floor with a *splat* and pointed at the sledgehammer. "What do you do with that?"

I glanced at the tool, then said, "There's someone in my wall."

"*Who* in the wall?" he repeated, brow furrowed.

"I'm going to find out."

"Have you been drinking?" Aubrey asked.

"Bring my sledgehammer back," the super called. He'd hardly taken a step out of the doorway when there was a loud *clank* from the laundry room, and then a current of water flowed out of the threshold. He yelped and ran inside.

I turned and finished hiking to the first floor and then hurried up the stairs. "I think there's an old lady in my wall,"

I told Aubrey.

There was a very loud silence over the line, before Aubrey said with a somberness I rarely heard from him, "That doesn't make any sense."

"*You* found a person in a wall," I protested.

"A skeleton. A very old skeleton. And that was different."

"It's not," I replied. "An old lady in the wall makes more sense than it being a ghost or a banshee."

"It actually doesn't. Say those words again. Slowly."

"I think there's an old lady in my wall."

"Your building is a hundred-year-old multiuse in the East Village. Suffice it to say, you probably have rats. Isn't there a coffee shop next door?"

"It's not rats."

"How would an old lady get in your wall?"

"How did Fortunato?" I countered.

"*What?*"

"Someone is screeching in the wall," I explained, reaching the fourth floor in a rush and out of breath. "No one believes me, but I'm going to prove it."

"Screeching?" Aubrey repeated. "Hang on, Sebastian, it's not a person, it's—"

I hung up and pocketed the phone as I reached our apartment. As I let myself in, Dillon warily backed up all the way to the middle of the front room, looking like he was ready to bolt to the loft at the first sign of insanity. I raised the sledgehammer in both hands, angled myself to one side, and then whaled on the wall to the right of the door. I immediately put a hole in the drywall, and the screeching started anew. Drawing back, I tried to put a second hole beside the first, but wildly missed. I was legally blind—what the hell did I expect? I'd made a third hole by the time Super had reached the open doorway, shouting in both English and Russian for me to stop.

"You crazy man!" he said, grabbing the handle of the sledgehammer and ripping it from my grasp. "How do I explain this to landlord? *Huh*? He will—"

Hissing emitted from the thrashed wall, cutting Super's tirade short, and we both looked toward the sound.

My phone was vibrating. I blindly retrieved it, tapped Accept, and said, "Yes?"

"It's an opossum, you bitch," Aubrey shouted over the line. Then he hung up.

Super approached the damage, broke off some drywall hanging like a jagged tooth, and poked his head in. He removed his own phone, turned on the flashlight, and studied the space between the inner and outer wall. "Opossum," he stated. "She's stuck down here and—" He leaned in farther, angled toward the loft. "Babies. She can't reach babies."

"It's really an opossum?"

"Come see."

I warily approached and glanced through the hole as Super stepped aside for me. "Son of a bitch…."

"You are lucky. I would have to make hole to get her out anyway."

I glanced at his glowering expression. "Please don't tell Boyfriend."

ROGER, HOUSTON

—

After *The Mystery of the Bones*
POV: Sebastian Snow

—

We were going to Los Angeles for our honeymoon.

Granted, we'd tied the knot in December and it was now May, but I've never enjoyed being rushed into things. I also don't enjoy long-distance travel or any location that boasts a UV index higher than five on the average, but I was a married man now, and the secret to a happy partner was compromise.

Compromise, red-tinted contacts, sunglasses, and SPF 100.

To be honest, as much as I grumbled about leaving the Emporium, Max's capable care beside the point, about spending serious cash on airfare and hotels, or about packing, which was its own particular torture and probably a circle Dante left out of his account of his travels through Hell, I was actually looking forward to a week-long vacation with Calvin. If Durango had taught me anything, it was that having nothing to do but eat, fuck, and visit historical locations was the true dream of every hedonist and I needed to embrace that.

But there'd been a delay leaving La Guardia—something about fueling, which Calvin insisted happened from time-to-time, and then there'd been turbulence, which, for a guy only flying for the second time in his life, was still terrifying, so when we got to Dallas/Fort Worth for our connection, we were late and stuck in air traffic. Needless to say, by the time we'd landed, we'd wildly missed our plane to LA and were informed there were no connecting flights with seat availability until the next morning.

I was a little grumpy about the whole situation, but that was mostly hunger, I'd surmised. I was technically on vacation, so I was doing my best to go with the flow of life—and the airline was providing vouchers for a nearby hotel, which seemed just fine. At least, that's what was offered to the first dozen customers in line at the gate counter being manned by a lone and frazzled attendant. The woman before us was now throwing a literal fit when it came to be known that the attendant had run out of vouchers and had nothing else to offer stranded travelers.

"*Great,*" Calvin muttered under his breath. He pulled his phone from his pocket, did a quick bit of typing one-handed, then passed it to me. "Give this hotel a call, baby. Book us a room for the night."

"What's a few hundred more bucks between friends?" I tapped the number Calvin had brought up on the reservation page and put the cell to my ear.

"I recently turned forty-four. I'm not sleeping in a chair at the gate," he answered before approaching the counter when Soccer Mom stormed off in disgust, still waving her hands and shouting obscenities over her shoulder. Calvin was much more polite with the agent as he went about rebooking us on flights for tomorrow.

A young man, way too perky for nine at night, answered my call. "Valley Resort and Convention Center. My name is Derek, how may I assist you?"

As a native New Yorker, I was immediately on edge by Derek's "Everything Is Bigger in Texas" manners. "Er, yeah, hi. I wanted to get a room for the night."

"*Oh!*" I could practically hear the wince in his tone. "We are completely sold out of our standard, two queen beds—"

"What about a king bed?" I interrupted.

I could hear tapping on a keyboard before Derek said, "I'm very sorry. Our resort is completely sold out. We have two conferences in town, and it's just been *crazy*."

"I see."

"Hm-mm. The International Clown Convention—"

"That must be a sight."

"—And the Kiss a Ginger Conference," Derek finished.

I glanced at Calvin as he made small talk with the attendant. "I'm married to a ginger. Will that get me a room?"

Derek laughed politely, automatically. "I'm afraid not. These rooms have been booked for months."

"Well, damn."

More tapping on a keyboard. "*Actually….*" And he drew the word out. "I do have one deluxe suite still available."

"That sounds expensive, Derek."

"Six hundred for the night. But it has a view of the atrium, a marble bathroom, private Jacuzzi, champagne service—"

"That sounds amazing, and maybe the clown industry makes that kind of money, but I'll have to pass."

"So sorry we couldn't do business with you, sir. Have a pleasant evening."

I grumbled some nicety, hung up, and stepped forward to tuck the phone into Calvin's pocket. "They're full-up."

Calvin glanced at me while taking our updated tickets from the attendant. "Every room? It's a convention center."

"Yeah, well, lots of clowns and redheads in town." Both he and the woman were staring at me. I waved a hand. "Two unrelated events. There was a suite available, but if there's a single moment in our entire marriage I can be a scrooge about money—let it be this one. I'm not paying six hundred and miscellaneous taxes to spend the night on a borrowed mattress."

Calvin tapped the tickets against the counter a few times. "We'll have to find a hotel farther away, I guess."

"I, um, might have a solution," the woman piped up. She smiled timidly when we both looked at her, and said, "Mission Operations. We don't have a business relationship, so it'd still be out-of-pocket, and I'm not even sure they have availability, but it's worth a try."

"Mission Operations," Calvin repeated.

She nodded quickly. "It's a pod hotel here in the airport."

"What is a pod hotel," I asked, but the question came out flat.

"It's neat," the attendant insisted. "A mini hotel, really." She pointed discreetly and added, "Head this way—Zone B. It's past the Jamba Juice on your left."

Calvin thanked her and took the handle of our suitcase in one hand. I reached for his other, and he accepted before leading the way out of line.

I know I said I was a homebody and that was why I didn't travel outside of the city, but honestly, it was the near-crippling anxiety I felt when going to unfamiliar, public locations that kept me in New York. Big, bright places like airports washed out my vision—then I really was blind, and not merely from a legal standpoint. I can't read signs very well and require my walking stick, and it was a stimulation overload because I found myself depending a lot more on my hearing to get around. The city might be home to nine million people, but it was a place of routine behavior. And when I *did* need public transport, I'd memorized all of the subways and stops. I was rarely thrown a curveball I couldn't immediately adjust to and I never had a situation that required driving.

But here?

I'd be so fucking freaked out if I were alone. I mean, were there signs for Zone B? I hadn't seen one—but was that because I'd simply missed it or literally couldn't see it? What if this pod hotel had no availability and I'd had to go to a hotel twenty miles away? Dallas was a big city, so I was certain Uber and Lyft were available no matter the time of day, but what if I were somewhere more isolated and the only way to get around was to rent a car? I'd be stranded.

Calvin knew all of this now. He'd long ago learned my limitations and my hang-ups, but he also knew I'd adapted and managed for thirty-four years, and I didn't need someone "more able" to rush to my aid. He knew I had methods for living in the world, and that if I did need help, I was capable of making it known. I didn't always ask with words—maybe that was in part due to the teases and taunts I endured as a kid and not wanting to draw attention to myself—but Calvin understood. The other week I'd handed him a carton of coffee creamer, and he read the expiration date aloud and gave it back. That was it. No explanation from me and no pity from him.

So moments like this—when I held a hand out and he simply took it and started walking? I could feel my anxiety ease with each step. I'd be fine here, because Calvin would help and not make me feel less of myself for it.

We walked down a long—very long—passage of mostly empty gates and shops shuttered for the evening. The wheels of our suitcase echoed on the polished floor, and the overhead speaker system played a canned safety announcement. Calvin gently tugged me to the side just before one of those buggy golf carts honked and zoomed past. Eventually we reached the Jamba Juice in question, the lights off and gate pulled down over the entrance. Calvin took the left as the hall branched in a few different directions, and we came to a stop outside a sort of incognito setup behind a glass wall.

"Mission Operations," Calvin read from a blinking neon sign overhead.

"Beam me up."

He smiled as the glass door automatically opened with a sort of *whoosh* sound effect. We had to adjust to single file down a narrow corridor that ended with a check-in counter and a lone employee, all of it obscenely backlit in some, I guessed, futuristic space aesthetic.

The guy sitting at the counter glanced up from his phone, sighed audibly as he pushed it aside, and said with such a bored tone that he might as well have been unconscious, "Welcome to Mission Operations."

I looked around Calvin's hulking figure and answered, "Houston sent us."

Calvin shot me a look. "Don't antagonize," he whispered. Then he turned back to the counter and the apathetic astronaut. "Do you have any rooms available?"

"You don't have a reservation?"

"No," Calvin said, holding up a finger when I opened my mouth, like he could just sense the smartass remark I had ready to let fly.

Astronaut sighed again, directed his attention to the monitor on his right, and said after a moment, "We have one pod currently available."

"Great." Calvin reached for his wallet.

"It's by the hour," the astronaut continued.

"So like a love hotel," I replied.

"Shush," Calvin murmured before saying, "We'll take it until seven."

Astronaut shifted to one side on his stool in order to look back and forth between us. "You're going to share?"

"Sharing is caring," I told him.

Astronaut didn't seem to think this was a great idea, but eventually shrugged, ran Calvin's credit card, passed him the room key, and wished us luck.

I followed Calvin through another automatic door to the right and down an even narrower hall, barely the width of our suitcase. On either side were tiny doors with one round window, giving even more credence to the space station theme. They alternated between two steps down and two steps up so as to fit as many *pods* into the limited real estate as possible.

"I'm becoming suspicious of why he wished us luck," I said quietly, mindful of the occupied rooms around us.

Calvin stopped outside pod sixteen, scanned the card, and the door popped open. He pushed it back, and the sound that escaped him was a combination of a grunt and disbelieving laugh. "I get it now." He walked forward, awkwardly maneuvering the suitcase in alongside. As Calvin turned to look at me, he stooped a little, and I realized that his six feet and change was flirting with the ceiling.

The pod was maybe five feet deep. *Maybe*. The bed— one of those smart designs—was currently in a sitting position, which allowed for enough leeway at the end to wriggle around it, shove the suitcase into the farthest corner, and then slide sideways into the bathroom. Although, calling it a bathroom implied it was an actual room. Which it was not. The stall was separated by a glass wall and nylon curtain for the shower. The sink and toilet were in there too. It took "combination" to a whole new level.

I clasped a hand over my mouth as a laugh escaped. "What the fuck?" I whispered, trying hard to rein myself in before travel-delirium got the best of me.

Calvin went to the bathroom stall, turned sideways to get between the toilet and wall in order to examine the complimentary soaps, and conked his forehead against the showerhead. He swore.

I stepped into the pod and shut the door. "Are you sure about this?"

"It'll work," he insisted, rubbing his forehead while stepping back into the—erm—bedroom portion of the pod. "I'm going to shower." Calvin bent at the waist to tug his T-shirt off, in order to avoid knocking his arms against the ceiling.

I sat on the mattress and picked up a flyer from the pillow that explained the room's amenities. "Don't give yourself a concussion."

Calvin kicked off his Vans, unbuckled his belt, and shimmied free from his jeans and boxer briefs before he managed to get his hulking frame and magnificent ass back into the shower. The curtain was yanked into place, and then the water started.

"Mission Operations sells sandwiches," I called over the spray. "You hungry?"

"Yes."

I stood, grabbed the room card, and said, hand on the doorknob, "Hey. It's a good thing we like each other."

"Why's that?"

"That mirror over the sink offers a very candid view of your balls."

Calvin shifted and put his middle finger in front of his dick for me to see via the reflection.

I laughed and made my way back to the front desk.

Mission Operations' own Jack Lousma was busily tapping away on his phone—the volume turned up and the clashes, bangs, and roars of victory suggesting all was well on the space station and that he had time to indulge in video games. He glanced up as I passed through the automatic door. "I only have the one pod," he stated.

"Yeah, it's small," I agreed. "The flyer said you sold food?"

Jack paused his game, sighed again while sliding off the stool, then opened the door on a refrigerated unit behind him. "I've got a pastrami or tuna sandwich."

A pastrami sandwich in a Texas airport certainly wasn't going to be like sitting down for lunch at Katz's, but the idea of canned fish in that closet-sized room with no windows? "Two pastramis," I said.

Jack looked over his shoulder. "No. I've got one pastrami and one tuna."

Dear God. Which of us got to eat the shitty, overpriced pastrami sandwich was really going to be the moment in which my commitment to Calvin would be judged?

"Did you want the one?" Jack asked.

I pinched the bridge of my nose and muttered, "Yeah. Just… give me a second. I'm trying to decide how much I love my husband."

Jack Lousma must have read something in my expression—read that the hunk who had muscles to feed was going to get the sandwich and we both knew it—and maybe he felt bad, imagining me choking down bland tuna on a soggy bun, because with a few more dramatic sighs, he fetched a cup of ramen from a nearby shelf, and after I asked about candy, sold me a Snickers too.

When I returned to pod sixteen, I found Calvin sitting at the foot of the bed, naked but for a pair of boxer briefs, flipping through channels on the super-slim television mounted to the wall.

"Good God," I said as the door clicked shut behind me. "There's a wet and mostly naked man in my room."

A smile tugged at Calvin's mouth. He leaned back on one hand and offered an absolutely shameless view of his ripped abs. "You didn't order a singing telegram?"

I tugged my sunglasses down an inch—for the dramatic effect, since I actually couldn't see shit by doing so. "I'm very curious what sort of song pairs with this look."

Calvin eased himself to his feet, head cocked to one side because of the ceiling, and met me in about a step and a half. "Happy Birthday, Mr. President."

"My birthday isn't for a few months."

Calvin looked thoughtful, then shrugged. "I must have the wrong room." He stepped around me.

"Whoa, hey, it can be the right room."

"Can it?"

"For, like, fifteen—*twenty* minutes. Until my husband comes back."

Calvin kissed me, then took the plastic bag as he sat again. "What'd you get?"

"Cockblocked." I stepped between his legs, went around to the left side of the bed, where there was a small electric kettle on a tiny shelf jutting out from the wall, and filled it with tap water.

He chuckled, asking, "Only one sandwich?"

"It's for you." I plugged the kettle in, then sat beside him. "But I'll take my Snickers."

Calvin passed the candy to me before unwrapping his sandwich and taking a bite. "Mm. Nothing like day-old, mass-produced deli sandwiches to remind you of college."

"I was more of the chicken-tenders-and-french-fry diet."

"School cafeteria?" Calvin asked between bites.

"Meal card," I agreed. "Had to get the most bang for my buck."

"I lived off bodega food. There was a sweet spot of about twenty minutes in the evenings where the owner would sell me any leftover sandwiches or bagels at a discount."

"We'd have been friends in college, I think."

"Except you were in grade school when I was studying constitutional law."

"Okay, but when you're really vague like that, our age difference comes across as weird." I stuffed what was left of the Snickers in my mouth, grabbed the cup of ramen, and went to the kettle.

"It's true, though." Calvin started flipping through what sounded like infomercials once again.

"Let's have age comparison guidelines."

"Like?"

"Like the threshold is my first hand job."

"Why is Ethan Cohen your threshold?"

I returned to the bed, stirring the unappealing noodles with a plastic fork. "I think if I was old enough to have my junk touched by someone else, it's less weird."

"All right." Calvin ate a piece of pastrami that had fallen out from between the bread, looked at me, and said, dead serious, "I was getting shot at overseas when you experienced your first dick-chafe."

"Only compare ages since we met?"

"Good idea." He gave me a quick kiss.

I took a shower afterward, and had just finished brushing my teeth and taking out my contacts when Calvin said, "There's... a problem with the bed."

I fumbled, grabbed my glasses, and put them on as

I turned. Calvin was lying on the bed, now in a horizontal position, with his feet hanging over the end. I snorted.

"Sebastian."

I cleared my throat and climbed onto the bed. I was practically on top of Calvin because there was simply not enough width for two full-grown men to lie on their backs side-by-side. "I don't think you were their ideal clientele when they were conceptualizing this place."

Calvin was frowning. He raised his hand and pointed a finger at me. "Don't laugh."

"I'm *not*."

He narrowed his eyes. "I know you're going to."

I shook my head and managed to mostly swallow a second snort.

"I will spank your ass so hard, you won't be able to sit comfortably on tomorrow's flight," he warned.

"Is that a promise?"

Calvin growled. He held my waist, yanked me closer, and kissed me hard. He slipped his hand underneath the hem of my T-shirt, his fingertips feverish—the whorls of his fingerprints all but burning their pattern into my flesh. He drew one leg up, slid it between mine, and rubbed his thigh against my dick.

I ran my fingers through Calvin's thick, still-damp hair before giving it a light tug. I asked between kisses, "Is this the honeymoon part of the trip?"

"You better believe it." Calvin shifted, using his bulk to move me onto my back.

"You don't want to wait until we're in Los—*oh my God!*" I yelped as I'd rolled with Calvin's motion… then kept rolling right off the side.

Calvin grabbed my bicep and jerked me toward him just before I crashed to the floor. He pressed me against his body, muttering, "This pod is like trying to fuck in an obstacle course."

"I'm not all that limber, plus I failed gym class in high school," I said, tilting my head in order to meet Calvin's eyes. "Let's hold off until we have considerable more real estate to roll around on."

ANDREW & LIAM

—

After *The Mystery of the Bones*
POV: Sebastian Snow

—

Louis Armstrong's trumpet began to play on the record player in the front room, followed by Ella Fitzgerald's scatting, and then quite possibly the most beautiful and perfect duet in jazz history began to sing "Dream a Little Dream of Me." I adjusted the volume a bit, then returned to the kitchen, where the polar opposite musicians could be heard just right. Calvin had been cooking all day in preparation of Thanksgiving, and the limited counter space had been cleared so he could work in relative ease. Despite the holiday being us and my father, who was due to arrive in an hour or so, you'd have thought Calvin was feeding an entire damn platoon. Roast duck, vegetarian-stuffed sweet potatoes, red curry squash soup, salad, fresh dinner rolls and cranberry sauce, and *pies*.

He'd baked two pies before I'd even showered and dressed that morning, and they had since been taunting me from the shelf beside the fridge.

I'd have said something about all the food, but hell, it wasn't like we wouldn't eat it. And I'd send Pop home with some too. This was all a direct result of Calvin's year and a half in therapy. He and his therapist had, pretty early on, discussed the need for a hobby. When I'd met Calvin, he didn't have one, unless you considered occasional bouts on his PlayStation a hobby. He only worked and sometimes slept. She had suggested a process-oriented hobby—that it wasn't so important the quality of the end result, but that the steps and methods of production were followed—to basically help Calvin turn off and give himself a chance to relax.

So when we'd moved in together and he finally had a real kitchen, it seemed only natural that Calvin try his hand at cooking. And then baking. Both of which I was thrilled over, because I was deemed the Official Taste-Tester in the house. I had offered to help today, though, but Calvin knew I hated cooking, so he'd suggested I clean the apartment. And when that was done, I cracked open the wine he'd bought, because it was five o'clock somewhere, and returned to his side at the counter.

I put a hand on Calvin's back and rubbed absently. "How's it coming in here, Martha?"

He smiled while chopping several cloves of garlic and slicing a lemon. "Not bad, Rachel." He collected the pieces and stuffed them into the duck's backside.

"Sure hope you took him out prior to plowing him," I said before sipping the wine.

"Of course I did. We took a romantic walk through Union Square Greenmarket," Calvin said. "Bought some goat cheese, the local wine my husband has already opened—"

"You said I could."

"Which is why I bought three," he continued, securing the back legs with twine. "I was going to pass on the flowers for said husband, but the duck thought it was a wise investment."

Calvin had come home from the chaos of the farmer's market yesterday with bags of food, but also a bouquet of carnations—peach-colored, he'd said—and they were now in a vase on the set table in the front room. He did that sometimes, just came home with flowers. Usually from a bodega, nothing special, but it always had a way of making me feel like a million bucks.

"Good thing you listened to the duck," I answered.

"Hm-hm. I know you like flowers." He leaned sideways and kissed me.

"Carnations," I corrected.

"Only."

"Don't tell anyone."

"I wouldn't dream of it." Calvin opened the oven and slid the duck in. He then turned his attention to scooping roasted squash from the rinds and dumping the flesh into a blender.

I looked at the glass in my hand and swirled the pinot grigio absently. Neither of us were big wine drinkers—beer was the alcohol of choice in our house—but 'tis the season and all. I did like how Calvin's freckles popped on his face when he drank wine. He said it always gave him a flush. I thought it was cute.

"Can I get you some wine?" I asked. "It's pretty good."

"Sure, baby. Thanks."

I grabbed a second glass from an overhead cupboard and poured a bit for Calvin. "Here you go."

Calvin took the glass, then tapped it against my own. He took a sip while eying me, then asked, "What?"

"What, what?"

"You've got your thinking crease."

I immediately rubbed between my eyebrows, saying, "I wish you guys wouldn't call it that."

Calvin added some liquid ingredients to the squash, blended it into a total pulp, then prompted with, "Well?"

"I think it's a Point A to Point Q situation," I warned.

He stirred a bit of water into a pot of popping cranberries and sugar, then motioned for me to continue.

"I was thinking, we haven't had wine in a while. Then I thought about your alcohol flush and I like it because it makes your freckles more… freckle-y."

Calvin laughed under his breath.

"Your freckles suit your face structure. They make you *look* like a Calvin…. Then I wondered why most people's middle names don't match their appearance or personality, but I figure it's because lots of middle names are chosen for familial reasons—like, Andrew was my dad's uncle's name. He passed in the Korean War. But Liam somehow suits you. Like the freckles. In fact, I think it's the freckles that make Liam work. They sort of complement the emotion in that name. And then—"

"Freckles brought you back to the wine and you offered me a glass," Calvin concluded. He added a bit of lime to the curry squash.

"Right. Wow, you followed that?"

"I speak Sebastian Andrew Snow fairly fluently."

"Don't be a smartass."

"Pot, have you met my kettle?" Calvin laughed when I started to bluster. He set his spoon down, wrapped his arms around me, and kissed my mouth, leaving the bite of wine on my lips.

"*But*, when you put Andrew together with Liam, we sound like completely different people," I said. "Like… like interior designers, living in Park Slope, with two-point-five children."

"That is extremely specific."

"Yeah. I don't like it."

Calvin shook his head. "Me neither."

"Let's leave them out of this," I finished.

"You brought them up."

"It's the wine. It's getting to my head. I'm *un*bringing them up."

Calvin kissed me again. "Sebastian and Calvin it is."

THE GOOD IN THE WORLD

—

After *The Mystery of the Bones*
POV: Calvin Winter

—

I tapped the key fob. The Ford Fusion's headlights blinked, the locks engaged, and the alarm chirped. That one note seemed to bounce off building façades and ricochet throughout the East Village. Even in the most populated city in the country, late-night blizzards had a way of silencing humanity. Like a television set to mute. Wet, heavy snow had been blanketing the roads, sidewalks, cars, and fire escapes for hours, and it had a way of making a man feel very… alone.

As if I were the only living human on the island of Manhattan.

With memories as my only company.

And wasn't that a special kind of hell? Just me and my nightmares, walking the beat on deserted streets. Forever, maybe.

All those atrocities that I couldn't escape, that therapy didn't erase, only tempered. The cruelty, the abuse, the death that humans inflicted upon one another. Horrors experienced firsthand, resting below the surface, waiting for the cold sweats and midnight tears to lower my defenses so that they could make me forget that where I was in the here and now was safe and secure.

I shook myself violently, like a dog coming in from the rain. I tried so hard to never bring that sense of hopelessness home. I took a deep breath and let the cold air expand my lungs, clean out the darkest corners inside me. I watched the falling snowflakes reflect in the tungsten glow of the overhead streetlamps, listened to the rumble of a street plow a block away, felt the weight of my holstered pistol pressing against my ribs. And when I was as close to human as I'd be that night, I unlocked the front door of the multiuse building and made my way up to 4B.

The living room lamp was on as I let myself inside our apartment.

Dillon, comfortable in his dog bed, raised his head. His tail thumped against the hardwood, but I made a motion for him to remain where he was, and he obeyed.

I quietly shut and locked the door, hung my winter and suit coats up, then crouched to untie my wet oxfords and leave them behind so I didn't track melting snow across the front room.

Sebastian was asleep on the couch, leaning sideways against the back cushions and hugging an overstuffed pillow to his chest. He looked as if he'd spent the night staring out the window behind the couch.

Taking careful steps across the room, avoiding the known floorboards that groaned with age, I stopped in front of the couch, leaned over Sebastian, and tugged the curtains shut. I took a moment to study my husband, touch his bristly jaw with the pad of my thumb, trace the tungsten band on his left hand. The ring sat a little loose on his finger, but was held in place by his big knuckle.

Sebastian had beautiful hands. I mean, aesthetically they were nice—soft from a lifetime of handling nothing more dangerous than an antique book of questionable poetry with cloth gloves. "Because cotton is a neutral material," he'd once explained to me. "It doesn't react with the surface or leave fingerprints." But his hands were beautiful to me because they had never known violence. The preservation of history didn't stain his hands, didn't leave remnants like blood and gunpowder did. I'd caught him making comparisons in the past—that his hands weren't masculine enough, that *he* wasn't masculine enough.

But I don't think Sebastian realized just how much courage it took to not fall into the cesspool of toxicity that exists for most men. By refusing to hide who he was, being unapologetic of his interests, and pursuing an education and career my own father would have tossed me to the curb for, Sebastian really was a living embodiment of strength. And if strength was an indicator of masculinity, then he had it in spades.

I enclosed my hand around Sebastian's, leeching warmth from his skin and into my numb fingers. It was nights like this, when I came home after midnight, feeling battered and broken, knowing that no matter how many awful scumbags I put away, it would never stop, that there would always be someone worse, someone more depraved. That another knife was driven into me, blade wedged into my back, and my armor so heavy that I felt like I couldn't take another step, like I'd finally collapse and not get up again….

I think how lucky I am that Sebastian saved my life. I think how I'd take a million more knives to the back if it meant shielding him from everything awful. And then I think…. I'll fight again tomorrow.

Because there's still a little good in this world.

ST. LOUIS WHAT NOW?

—

After *The Mystery of the Bones*
POV: Sebastian Snow

—

Cab Calloway was singing over the shop speakers, keeping me company as I stood at the counter, sifting through old Christie's catalogues, hunting for toy trains. Let me rephrase. I wasn't looking for a specific tinplate toy to bid on, considering these booklets were years out-of-date. I was looking for the actual photographs of collections that'd once upon a time been for sale. My client collected professionally taken *pictures* of *toy* trains, which was an extremely… *specific hobby*. But considering I was the man who'd lost his goddamn mind last month after coming into possession of a nineteenth century surgeon's bloodletting set, I was not one to judge the passions of others.

Anyway. He wanted to pay for old catalogues and I

wanted to finally get rid of them, so it seemed an easy way to pass the time while Max was on his lunchbreak.

The bell over the door chimed as it was opened. Two distinct treads entered the Emporium. I flipped the page.

"You're the guy."

I raised my head, pushed my glasses up, and studied a curious pair. A middle-aged man and woman—each wearing enough of what I assumed to be rainbow paraphernalia that they could be mistaken as grand marshals for the city's Pride parade. My brows knitted together, and I said, "I'm one of four million guys. You might need to be more specific."

They looked at each other and immediately broke into a fit of giggles.

I straightened from my hunch over the catalogues, set my hands on the counter, and asked, "Can I help you with… something?"

"You're *the* guy," the man said, emphasizing *the* like it cleared up our miscommunication entirely. "The gay one."

"Wow. We've narrowed your search down to a population of about seven hundred thousand."

The woman, still giggling, said, "He means you're the gay detective. The one who moonlights as an antique dealer."

"Oh." I felt a blush rising to my cheeks. "Yes. I mean— no. It's the other way around. And I'm retired from that. Detecting. I wasn't even a detective."

They both smiled and in unison, exclaimed, "Amateur sleuth!"

"Er—busybody is probably more—"

"We read about you," the woman continued without missing a beat.

"Do I have a Wikipedia page?"

"The news called you New York City's gay Miss Marple."

"Wait, hang on, the media compared me—"

"After you saved your detective boyfriend and stopped a serial killer last Christmas," the man interjected.

I looked at him and slowly corrected, "Husband. And it was two Christmases ago." My gaydar was nonfunctional most of the time, but the way his face lit up at my response—dude was hella gay.

"Detective Snow," he said.

"Winter," I corrected again. "I'm Snow."

"Hyphenated?" the woman asked.

I glanced back at her. "Ampersand. Sorry, *who* are you?"

"Marilyn Goldman," she said, reaching a hand out for mine and shaking enthusiastically.

"I'm Zachary Coletti," her partner said next, snatching my hand and sandwiching it between both of his in a way that made my skin crawl. New Yorkers had an average of three inches of personal space, and the double handshake *always* burst that hard, fought-for bubble.

I tugged my hand free.

"We're on vacation," Marilyn explained. "From St. Louis."

"I'm sorry." The jab came out like a knee-jerk reaction.

"We wanted to visit all things queer in the Big Apple," she continued, thankfully oblivious to my remark.

"Uh-huh. Well, I'm sorry to disappoint you, but the Emporium isn't a gay-centric shop."

"You're gay," Zachary answered, like maybe I didn't know.

"I'm not for sale."

"Just my luck," he said with a sort of wicked shy smile.

I cleared my throat and said, desperate to fill the bizarre silence, "I mean… I do have a few daguerreotypes of what I'm quite certain are lesbian couples."

Marilyn and Zachary exchanged looks again.

"I spoke with a professor at Columbia last week about them. He insisted they were roommates. I swear to God, the photo could have been two women naked and embracing in one bed, and he'd have defended a dissertation on the familiarity of female friendships."

Marilyn and Zachary both gasped at the same time.

I startled and cut short my rant. "What?"

"And there was *only one bed*!" they both exclaimed at once.

"What—?"

"It's my favorite trope," Zachary explained.

"Same," Marilyn agreed, nodding. She asked me, "Do you read romance books?"

That heat was back, crawling up my neck, across my face, making my skin feel like little pinpricks of light were going to shoot out of every pore. "Well, I, uh—I prefer mysteries." They were both staring at me, and I felt like my face was about to combust at this point. "Sometimes I do. The bookshop next door—"

"Queer books?" Marilyn interrupted.

"No. I mean, it's just a used bookstore, but sometimes the owner finds gay romances and lets me borrow them. I'm not really into hetero love affairs."

Zachary began vigorously tapping Marilyn's arm. "The flyer, Marilyn. Give him one. You brought them, right?"

She was already digging through the messenger bag hanging from her shoulder, the front covered in no fewer than three dozen buttons, although I couldn't make out what any of them were. Marilyn unearthed a slightly crumpled flyer and thrust it into my unwilling hands.

Awkwardly holding it and realizing neither had any intention of leaving my store until I acknowledged the contents, I sighed a little, reached for my magnifying glass, and read, "Queer Expectations." I glanced up. "After having Ethan Cohen's hand down my pants and liking it, I've not really had any other sort of expectation in life."

Zachary's mouth dropped open.

Marilyn rolled her finger in a motion for me to continue reading.

I returned to the flyer, and after a moment, concluded with, "Gay book convention." Not that I wasn't interested in LGBTQ studies or biographies—I mean, I *was* me. History and research were at the top of my list of pleasures, right beside a generous helping of cheesecake and Calvin smacking my bare ass and calling it pretty. But I have to admit, sometimes it's nice to get lost in a fictional story, and seeing oneself represented—

"It's specifically for romance books," Marilyn corrected.

I lowered the flyer and asked with what sounded like hopeful wariness, "There's enough gay romance books to warrant a convention?"

They both nodded in sync.

I brought the magnifying glass to the paper. "It's next month?"

"In St. Louis," Zachary concluded.

"*Oh.*" I heard the disappointment in my tone and decided to tuck it away to scrutinize at length once I was alone.

But if he heard the note of displeasure, Zachary ignored it. "St. Louis's LGBTQ community isn't even comparable to New York's—we know that. But we're on the top ten list for most gay-friendly cities in the country now."

"I'm not looking to move."

"And Pride draws a few hundred thousand every year."

"I'm a low-key gay. Usually celebrate Pride from my couch."

Zachary reached out and tapped the flyer so hard, he almost punched his finger through it. "But St. Louis was really the *perfect* location for Queer Expectations! Good food, good sights, equidistant from the East and West Coast…. They have all sorts of romance writers, you know. Historical, contemporary, mystery—"

"Are you two the organizers or something?"

Marilyn and Zachary beamed at what I guessed was a massive compliment, but said in unison, "We're volunteer staff."

"Ah." I politely offered the flyer. "Well, thanks for stopping by… I guess."

Zachary's expression dropped. "You're not interested?"

"It's not that. I just don't leave the city very often."

"B-but the romance books," Zachary tried, his voice almost cracking like a kid holding back tears.

"I have a vision condition," I tried. "I only travel if my husband can—"

"Bring him along."

Marilyn had her hands balled into fists and was shaking them excitedly at chest level. "Yes! Plenty of spouses come. He'd fit right in."

I swallowed and was a little surprised that it felt like a softball was lodged in my throat. Beth knew I enjoyed romances. It was sort of a back-and-forth thing between us. She'd really dug deep to find one I'd like and had won me over with a title about two gay cops that I'd since reread, like… eight times. Max had seen the paperbacks in my office over the last two years, even thumbed through them occasionally while slacking off, but I hadn't really ever… told anyone else. I'm not sure why. I wasn't ashamed of liking them. The ones Beth found me were really well-written stories. But I guess… that stigma of enjoying romance books was enough to make me hesitant. After all, I dealt with enough bullshit being gay and legally blind, and I had no control over those aspects of my life. I didn't need to advertise to strangers that there were even more ways to mock me.

"Keep the flyer," Marilyn insisted. "You know, just in case."

I looked at it a final time before folding it and sticking it in my back pocket. "Sure. Thanks."

"Can you tell us which way Stonewall is?" she asked next.

I sighed, more heavily this time. "You're in the wrong Village."

"Sorry I'm late," I said in a rush. I dropped my messenger bag to the floor, pulled out the seat across from Neil, and plopped down.

After everything that'd happened the last two years, from Neil nearly taking a bullet for me at Valentine's, to putting his badge and career on the line for Calvin during Christmas, to simply being my friend and supporting my marriage when I think he had some regret built up about not having taken that chance with me when we'd been together, Neil and I had an unspoken arrangement to meet for lunch once a week. Whenever his schedule could swing it. Just him and just me. Calvin knew, of course. I'd be an idiot to try to hide that I met my ex on the regular for tacos, but more importantly, there was *no reason* to hide it. Calvin understood, at least on an intellectual level, that it wasn't a love thing between Neil and me. At least, not romantic love. I did love him, but as a friend. Neil was my best friend, if I were being honest, and it wasn't because he'd seen me naked that I said this.

This was the relationship we'd always wanted to have—friends. And we had a lot of lost time to make up for.

"I'm quite used to it," Neil replied. He took a sip of water and then crossed his legs, somehow managing to display every square inch of his well-put-together body in an even more well-put-together suit.

"It's been a day."

"Aren't they all?"

"There's that." I leaned over, found my glasses in my bag, and exchanged my sunglasses for them.

"I ordered for you."

"What'd I get?"

"Kale salad with balsamic dressing on the side." Then the corner of Neil's mouth twitched upward. "God, your face. I'm kidding. Burger and fries."

"No tacos?"

"It's not Tuesday."

"It's like you forget I'm armed."

"What, your cane? You don't scare me. Last week, some guy tweaked out of his mind came at me on a scene, wielding a machete."

"Where'd he get a machete in New York City?" I asked.

"I'm glad *that's* what you've focused on in this story."

"You're obviously okay," I protested. "Sorry. Why didn't you tell me last week you almost got hacked?"

I don't pick up on the subtle body cues of most people—vision and all—but I'd had plenty of time to study Neil over the years, and I could deduce what was unspoken with him as well as I could with Calvin or my own father. The way Neil shifted, like he suddenly had no ass (Neil's ass was perfectly fine) and the seat was the shittiest piece of furniture he'd ever sat on—there was some serious unease bubbling under the surface. "What?" I asked.

"*What?*" he countered.

"No repetition."

"I'm just sitting here."

"Are you blushing?"

"You can't see blushes."

"That's why I'm asking."

Neil frowned. "No. I am *not* blushing," he said with the sort of finality Vader had when telling Luke he was his father.

I leaned forward. "Did you meet someone?"

"I keep the same hours as Winter."

"So you met him on the job?"

That shift again. "I didn't—"

"You couldn't tell me you'd nearly been butchered in the line of duty because you were… you know." I made a circle with one hand and slid my index finger in and out.

Neil pinched the bridge of his nose and took one of those long, count-to-ten breaths. When he'd finished, he opened his eyes and looked at me again.

"Hi."

"Why're you late?" he asked.

"Don't try to spin this conversation."

Neil leaned back and smoothed his tie, saying, "The burger was fifteen dollars."

I put my hands up. "Fine. Some customers, let's call them Frick and Frack, stopped by the Emporium looking for a Real Gay to play tour guide."

Neil raised one eyebrow. "The Emporium is half a dozen blocks away from a bar where patrons have sex in the bathrooms with male go-go dancers, and customers zeroed in on you for the gay experience?"

"What's that supposed to mean?"

"You're wearing mismatching loafers."

I looked down. "Son of a bitch, again?"

"And before you ask, yes, it's obvious."

"What is?" I asked, raising my head.

"When you're late for work. Because of… how'd you put it.…" Neil raised his hands and inserted his index finger into the tunnel of the other.

I kicked Neil's shin, and he swore loud enough to earn a glare from a pair of old ladies in the booth to our right.

He reached down, rubbed his leg, and directed an apology their way. "You're a salty shit," he hissed at me.

"Better turn that frown upside down, Neil. Not all men appreciate what a grouchy fuck you are."

He straightened in his seat. "There *isn't* a man."

"Sure."

"Seb."

"I said, sure."

"You said it with a tone."

"There was no tone."

"I swear to God."

I lifted up and tugged the folded flyer from my back pocket. "Not to interrupt your righteous indignation, but have you ever heard of Queer Expectations?" I cautiously unfolded the paper.

Neil reorganized his expression, took another one of those long, calculated breaths, then said, "One could argue, based on being a gay man, that all of our expectations are colored in that respect."

"What the fuck school of philosophy did you graduate from?" I asked.

Our waitress came around then, depositing two plates on the table—said burger for me, and—

"I thought you said no tacos."

"I did."

I pointed at Neil's plate. "Then what is that?"

"Tacos. For me. I was on time."

"This mystery man is going to kill you before the week's out," I grumbled.

Neil picked up a taco in one hand, gave me the finger with the other, and took a big bite.

I rolled my eyes, grabbed the ketchup bottle on the tabletop between us, and said while shaking it, "I'm not talking about anything akin to The Queer Experience. Just— Queer Expectations. It's an event."

Neil furrowed his brow, took another bite, then asked, "What sort of event?"

"It's… um… it's a book convention."

"Oh."

I pointed a french fry at him. "You thought it was some kind of sex thing, didn't you?"

"With a name like that…." He shrugged.

"So you haven't heard of it?"

"No. Should I?"

"No. I mean, I guess not."

"What sort of books?"

"Gay books."

Neil snorted. "No shit, Sherlock."

I stuck the fry in my mouth, smoothed out the flyer, and hesitantly offered it.

Neil took the paper. After a minute, his gaze rose to meet mine. "Romance books?"

I shrugged.

"Since when do you read romance?"

I shrugged again. "Since opening the Emporium and meeting Beth, I guess."

"When we were dating?"

I nodded.

"Huh." He passed the flyer back and indicated to it with a nod of his chin. "You going, then?"

"It's in St. Louis."

"Is St. Louis romantic?"

"The Midwest doesn't exactly conjure up feelings of true love," I answered, folding the paper, leaning to one side, and slipping it back in my pocket. "More like… corn."

"There's more there than corn."

"Jesus billboards, maybe."

"I meant," Neil began, and that stressed patience was back in his tone, "you could make a vacation out of it. The convention is right around Valentine's Day."

"But then I'd have to tell Calvin why I want to go to *Missouri*."

"I think he'd probably want a heads-up, yeah." Neil picked up a second taco before raising an eyebrow. "He doesn't know you read romance books?"

"Let's talk about something else."

"Why are you embarrassed?"

"I'm not."

"You're a shit liar."

I picked up my burger and took a huge bite. Too big, in fact. I had to chew with my mouth partially open.

Neil grimaced. "I can't believe you're married."

"Neither can I," I mumbled around the food. After swallowing, I said, "Did you know, after the Bones case, the media gave me a nickname?"

"Did they?"

"Yeah. Frick and Frack told me about it."

"What was it?"

"The gay Miss Marple."

Neil choked. He thumped on his chest a few times before he started laughing. Like, *really* laughing. He'd always had a nice laugh, and looked so much younger without the perpetual scowl on his face, but I sure as hell wasn't going to point that out while Neil was practically doubled over at my expense.

"Stop it."

"Oh my God."

"It's not that funny."

"Yes, it is." Neil put a hand over his eyes, but the attempt to collect himself was short-lived and he broke into another fit of giggles. "The gay Miss Marple."

"I am not Miss Marple. She was partially based on Christie's *grandmother*."

"Aren't you, like, eighty too?"

"And she knitted cardigans."

Neil raised an eyebrow and pointed. "What's that you're wearing?"

"Fashion, Neil."

"Looks like a cardigan to me."

"It was a hundred and fifty bucks at Macy's. And, for the record, Miss Marple was a thornback."

"I thought she was a spinster."

"Too old," I answered.

"Thornback sounds metal as hell."

I rolled my eyes to the ceiling. "I don't know why they didn't go with Hercule—"

"Because no one can pronounce his name," Neil interrupted.

"That's not my problem. He's a brilliant detective who

has dramatic denouements—"

"And you're a nuisance in frumpy sweaters. Miss Marple it is."

"I'm leaving." I grabbed my messenger bag, coat, and started for the door.

"Miss Marple, wait!"

"*Can it,*" I called over my shoulder.

He was still laughing. "We need your busybody gossip!"

I yanked open the door, turned, and said, loud enough that the entire restaurant might as well have been part of our discussion, "Maybe you'll be worth gossiping about if you ever get back to doing the horizontal refreshment."

"*Horizontal refreshment?*"

"Goodbye, Neil."

"See you next week, Miss Marple."

On the way back to the Emporium, I made a detour at Good Books. I walked inside just as Beth was squatting in front of a shelf jam-packed with biographies and not-so-carefully dropping a stack of books to the floor. "With your knees, Beth."

She straightened, looked over her shoulder, then huffed. "Don't be smart with me, Sebby."

"Seb."

"I bought bulk at an estate sale the other day—real cheap," she explained, pointing at the pile beside her feet.

"How cheap?"

"Like, five bucks a box."

"Good deal."

Beth scoffed while taking off her funky glasses. She wiped the lenses with the corner of her Ugly Christmas Sweater, worn about three weeks postholiday—a ridiculously fuzzy ensemble with a giant cat face, pompoms, and bells. She jingled while moving. "Yeah, well, that's what I thought, but I should have known it was too good to be true. Is Mercury in retrograde or something?"

"I have no idea. What's wrong with the books?"

"They were dropped off today." She put her glasses on, waved at what looked like a dozen boxes stacked against the wall near the door to her back room, then said, "They're all crafting books."

"What sort—?"

"*Everything*! Origami, crocheting, cabinet-making, basket-weaving, macramé, leatherwork, beer-making—"

I perked up. "Beer—"

But Beth was on a roll that would not be stopped. "Calligraphy, papier-mâché, cross-stitch, casting, floral designing—both Western arrangement and Japanese ikebana—"

A teenage girl was warily approaching, holding several books in her hands and looking like she wanted to pay but was unwilling to interrupt. Beth glanced at her, stomped to the counter—Crocs today, not Birkenstocks—and waved the kid over.

"Metalwork, glassblowing, *knifemaking*, Sebby."

"Uh-huh." I turned away from the counter, moved to the bulletin board near the door, and leaned in close to study the myriad of flyers for literature events happening in both the city and tri-state area.

"The market for craft and hobby books has tanked over the last few years, and now I have enough of them to fill a damn library. Would you like a bag?"

The girl squeaked out a response, and then the register dinged as the cash drawer shot open.

I pushed my sunglasses up and squinted at a familiar advertisement. "Frick and Frack stopped by to tell you about Queer Expectations, huh?" I tapped the flyer in question, tacked beside one for a live reading of Shakespeare's sonnets, all 154 of them, next Saturday in Central Park, come snow or shine, and another for a class being offered out in Jersey that was pretty self-explanatory: *Write F*cking Better!* And a phone number—ask for Desiree. Or maybe that didn't mean what I thought it did….

"The skaters?" Beth inquired.

The teen stepped around me, hurried out the door, and vanished into the cold afternoon.

"Not the literal Frick and Frack," I said, turning to Beth, who was still behind the counter.

"*Lady, Let's Dance* was one of my favorite movies when I was a girl," she said with a touch of serenity in her tone. "I wanted to be a figure skater when I grew up." Beth sighed, looked at me, then asked, "What the hell are we talking about?"

I tapped the flyer.

"Oh. Queer Expectations. What about it?"

"Did two very excited and festive individuals come in earlier to tell you about it?"

Beth raised an eyebrow and jingled as she left the register. "No. I'm on their mailing list."

"Have you gone?"

Beth nodded. "Last year. It's not bad. I don't think it's your scene, Sebby."

"But I like the books you loan me."

"There's a lot of attendees."

"Define *a lot*."

"Few hundred."

I grimaced.

"Lots of penises," she continued.

"Wait, like… actual…?"

She shot me a glare while leaning over the front of the counter and fumbling through a coffee mug full of pens without actually looking at it. "You're married to a total hottie."

"I'm well aware. But I can still appreciate the male aesthetic when presented with the opportunity."

Beth yanked a pen free and then came toward me with it. She waved it back and forth in front of my face—a bobble penis on top wriggled like an excitable puppy dog. "I meant this. Penis swag."

"I don't need penis swag."

"Well, I don't either, but you get it anyway."

"Can't I say, *no, thank you?*"

Beth lowered the pen and gave me the hairy eyeball. "As if you'd say, *no, thank you.*"

She was right. I was sort of an asshole, after all.

"Anyway," she continued, tossing the pen at the counter and completely overshooting. "If you can keep your grumpy sensibilities in check around crowds and explicit swag, maybe you'd enjoy it."

"Would I find more gay cop romances?"

"Without a doubt. Probably get the authors to autograph them too."

"It's a catch-22 situation," Max said, walking beside me as we left the Emporium for the evening.

I'd gone back and forth with myself all afternoon about the idea of attending the book convention. On the one hand, I never did stuff like that—indulging in an interest (that didn't take place at a crime scene) with strangers. It could be… fun. But on the other, I was a homebody, a workaholic, and I didn't like people enough to purposefully attend a large gathering of them in my free time. And when I thought I'd decided on my answer—a firm *no*—I circled right back to: *but I like books*. What if some author at Queer Expectations wrote about little old lady lesbian sleuths? Miss Butterwith, but super gay. I'd eat that with a spoon.

"A catch-22 is a problem where the solution is denied by the circumstance of the problem itself," I corrected.

"I know what a catch-22 is."

"But this isn't that. I just don't—"

"Like people. Like travel. Like spending money on yourself."

"Wow, you really do know how to sum me up into an appealing package," I said dryly. I gave Dillon's leash a tug when he stopped to inspect something smooshed into oblivion on the sidewalk.

"You need a vacation."

"I already took one."

"Last year," Max said, looking at me. "For your honeymoon."

I tugged my other hand from my coat pocket and waved it. "I wouldn't call it a honeymoon."

"No, I wouldn't either. Because it was, like, May. And you'd been married for half a year already." Max unzipped his coat pocket, tugged a hat free, and yanked it over his messy hair. "It's a catch-22 because you can't go to St. Louis without telling Calvin you like romance books, and since you refuse to tell Calvin you like romance books, you can't go."

"It's not that I *refuse*—"

"You do too."

"Christ, Max. It embarrasses me, all right?"

"Why?" He nudged my shoulder with his own. "I mean, seriously, Seb. You don't mind me knowing. Beth is practically your dealer."

"I told Neil," I mumbled into my scarf.

"You told Crankypants Millett? What'd he say?"

"Huh."

"What?"

I stopped beside a tree and let Dillon do his business. I glanced at Max and said, "Neil said *huh*."

"He's got such a way with words," Max said with a shake of his head. But then he pointed at me with a gloved hand. "Why won't you tell your husband?"

"Max—"

"Come on."

"I don't know," I said, hearing the frustration starting to grow in my tone. "It's… it's not the actual genre that embarrasses me. I've read some great stories. I'm proud of those authors. But there's the social stigma."

"Streaking has a social stigma too," Max pointed out. "I've still done it. Twice, actually."

I ignored that and finished with, "I've been laughed at enough in my life. I don't need to give society another reason."

"Fuck the Man," Max protested.

I looked at him.

"'The Man' in this context is society."

"I got it."

We started walking again, and when we reached the end of the block, Max said, "I say this because I love you, boss, but when you've gotten your head out of your ass, let me know the dates you'll be gone. Oh. Also, I read somewhere that St. Louis is famous for this cake called the gooey butter or something? Smuggle one back for me, and I won't even ask for time and a half for having to work alone."

I spared Max a look and tried to not sound overly interested while asking, "They're famous for cake?"

"St. Louis-style pizza, too."

"The fuck is *St. Louis-style pizza?*"

I unlocked the door to 4B, crouched to unclasp Dillon's leash, then stepped inside. I put my glasses on, set the messenger bag on the floor, and hung my coat and scarf on the rack.

"Hey, baby," Calvin called from the loft.

"Hey," I answered. I moved to the table-for-two and set my keys aside, fished the stupid flyer from my back pocket and smacked it down, then dropped the mail on top of it. "You're home early."

"Are you complaining?" Calvin answered, his voice near the closet on the opposite end of the room.

"Nope. Are you naked?"

I heard him chuckle. "Not anymore."

"Lame." I walked down the hall and entered the kitchen. I heard Calvin come down the stairs as I opened the fridge, fetched a beer, and popped the top off. "Remind me to call the electric company tomorrow," I said between long pulls.

"Why?" Calvin was somewhere in the front room.

"They mailed us another bill. That's three in two weeks. Not only is our account current, but we're set up to be paperless."

"All right."

"All childhood, you're anxious to grow up," I continued, opening the fridge again to grab a bottle for Calvin, "so you can do fun adult things, like drive or drink beer or fuck, and it turns out you spend all of your time following up with other disillusioned adults over crap like paperless electric bills."

Calvin poked his head into the kitchen as I moved to the sink. "You can't drive." Phone in one hand, he motioned at me with it. "And you're double-fisting beer right now."

"This one is yours," I answered, popping the top off the second bottle, but then taking a sip from it.

"Looks like it." He moved into the doorway, leaned against the threshold, and resumed tapping on his phone.

"I'm not fucking," I pointed out after a moment of silence had passed.

Calvin hummed absently.

"And the magic's gone," I concluded. "A year ago, you'd have been walking around the house naked for me."

"Not in January."

"Now is the winter of our discontent."

Calvin didn't look up from his phone as he asked in a very nonchalant tone, "Did you just compare my wearing jeans to having reached the depth of unhappiness?"

"I think so."

"When did you last eat?"

I remembered lunch with Neil—more specifically, the lunch I didn't finish—and frowned. "It's been a while."

"I think you're hangry."

"I'm not hangry," I protested, even though I very clearly was. "I'm frustrated."

"Hm-hm."

"Society forces us to deny what we derive pleasure in."

"Society has nothing to do with me wearing pants. I'm wearing them because it's cold." At that, Calvin tucked his phone into his pocket and looked up.

"I'm not talking about your pants. I'm talking about—there's this—*books*—" I stopped stumbling over myself when I felt my phone vibrate. I tugged it free, brought the screen close, and squinted at the notification.

Calvin Winter

FWD: Trip Confirmation – LaGuardia to St. Louis Lambert International.

I swiped to open the email.

You're all set! You can make adjustments to your itinerary by logging into your account. Thank you for flying with us.

Passenger Information:

Calvin Winter, Seat 2D

Sebastian Snow, Seat 2C

I looked up. Calvin had a cute, boyish smile on his face. "What's this?"

"An early Valentine's Day gift for my husband." Calvin pushed off the wall and walked toward me. "Because I know he's a big fan of schmoopy love, but has some kind of bug about admitting it." He put his hands around my waist and tugged me close.

"I don't have a bug."

"You have a bug," Calvin said again in a low, sexy voice before kissing my mouth lightly.

"You saw the flyer on the table."

"You bet your cute butt I did."

I felt my entire face warm. "Fine. I like romance books. Get your shots in."

"I know you like romance books."

"What?"

"I'm a detective. You think I don't know when you're lying?"

"But—so you went ahead and bought first-class airfare

to America's Breadbasket without consulting me? What if I had plans at work?"

"That'd be terrible," Calvin said in a placating tone before kissing me again. "You know, my sergeant approved a vacation request I'd put in for last week. I hadn't decided what to surprise you with, but that convention seems perfect. Talk about serendipitous."

"You could have bought flowers and taken me out for a candlelit dinner," I mumbled, sounding like a man who was well fucking aware of having lost the battle but nonetheless insisted on beating his dead horse.

"Just flowers?"

"And dinner."

Calvin nodded. "Okay." He took out his phone. "I'll cancel the flight and let my sergeant know—"

I grabbed his phone and held it out of reach. "You already went to all this effort."

"I have a cancellation policy on those seats." Calvin reached for the phone.

I bent back as much as I could, what with one of his hands still around me. "No, no. Your sergeant approved time off already. If you cancel the request, he'll blame me."

"Oh, I doubt that. It'll be fine." Calvin reached again.

I wriggled free and, while holding both phones, made for the hall. "Max was telling me about this cake St. Louis is famous for. Maybe I'd like to try that. And we might as well, you know, check out the romance convention while we're there. 'Tis the season and all." I turned in the doorway and glanced back.

Calvin had crossed his big buff arms over his chest and was smiling.

"So, I'll… register us as attendees."

Calvin nodded.

I walked away, then backtracked. "Calvin?"

"Yeah?"

"Thank you."

"You're welcome."

TROPE: ONLY ONE BED

—

After *The Mystery of the Bones*
POV: Calvin Winter

—

I stepped through the front door of 4B just as a high-pitched, erotic gasp sounded from the television, followed by a string of colorful cusses from my husband. Sebastian stood in front of the entertainment system, close to the screen, jabbing at the remote in one hand. I closed the door, threw the deadbolt, and met his gaze when he jerked his head up. "Hi."

"It's not what it sounds like."

I unbuttoned my pea coat. "Sounds like the Food Network."

Sebastian snorted and started vigorously punching buttons again. "If the end goal was a bun in the oven, yeah."

"Why're you watching straight porn?" I asked. I shrugged

the coat off, shook the snow from it, and set it on the rack beside the door. I crouched to take off my soaking wet shoes.

"I'm not. I'm looking for the Weather Channel."

"Ninety-three," I said, setting the oxfords beside the door and crossing the room, pausing to pat Dillon's head.

"Really?" Sebastian found the station and looked at me a second time as a meteorologist excitedly discussed the incoming Nor'easter. "I thought it was in the hundreds."

I shook my head.

He pointed at the television as he stepped around it to meet me at the loft stairs. "When did we sign up for a porn package?"

"We didn't, but that explains our last bill. I'll call them tomorrow."

"I don't even know who'd bother with cable porn these days," Sebastian continued. "It's all the same. Bodacious, barely legal babes and lusty, lonely housewives." He put a hand on the back of my neck and pulled me down into a kiss. "You're cold."

"I had to park half a dozen blocks away. Some asshole on our street took up two spots." I started up the stairs, with Sebastian trailing a few steps behind.

"You should have him towed."

"Not during a blizzard."

"The mayor declared a state of emergency for the city."

"I heard," I answered. I shrugged my suit coat off and tossed it to the bed. I unbuckled my shoulder holster and stored it in the closet, while Sebastian hovered at the stairs to my back. "Emporium closed tomorrow?"

"Yup."

I peeled my wet socks off and tossed them into the hamper with the rest of the dirty laundry.

"You know the pornos that begin with shitty setups?"

I glanced at Sebastian as I unbuttoned my shirt. "Like the repairman stopping by to fix the cable-dishwasher-vacuum cleaner?"

He nodded. "I never understood that. I mean, *I do*—introduce sexy characters so the viewer is invested for the entirety of the humping—but honestly, how decent of a job do the actors ever do?"

"They weren't hired for their grasp on the character's emotional arc, baby." I tossed the shirt into the basket and bit back a smile when Sebastian's gaze dropped and lingered on my bare skin.

"But do you know how much more appealing those introductions would be if they used classic romance tropes?" he asked upon looking back up.

"I do not."

"Like… meet/cute. Two guys bump into each other at a library and help pick up each other's books."

"Then have sex in the public bathroom?"

Sebastian shrugged. "Well, it *is* porn—we have to skip the first dates and meeting the parents."

"What else?" I finished undressing and reached for my pajamas, left on the bed from this morning.

"Amnesia. But that would be tricky with porn, because it's all about the characters falling in love again. Still, I think it'd be possible."

"You've thought about this more than once, haven't you?" Dressed in flannel pants and a T-shirt, I turned around.

Sebastian's cheeks, perpetually covered in a few days of whisker growth because the man just couldn't be bothered with any personal grooming beyond the bare minimum, were pink from a blush. It was cute. It was always cute, the way he'd get a little embarrassed or self-conscious, but then steamroll himself by forcing the conversation. We'd been together for two years and he still got hung up on sex-talk, or the recent disclosure of his enjoyment of romance books. But Sebastian always tried, always pushed forward. And in that respect, he would always be more courageous than me, whether he believed that or not.

"'Only one bed' is my favorite," Sebastian said instead of answering my question.

"That's a trope?"

"Yeah. Two characters forced to share a bed due to extenuating circumstances. We're actually in the perfect setup for that trope right now."

"Being married seems like a compelling reason to share a bed," I told him, moving close, setting my hands on his hips, and tugging Sebastian forward.

He rolled his eyes. "No."

"No?"

"That's not how the trope works. We're supposed to be forced to share because—for example—there's a blizzard that's trapped us in an isolated location and there's one bed and it's cold, so neither of us can be stubborn and sleep on the floor."

"So we're not supposed to be married in this situation?" I asked, for clarification.

"Right. Even better if, on the surface, we don't like each other." Sebastian patted my chest. "Like when we first met."

"You make it sound a lot worse than it was."

"You threatened to arrest me for being a smartass."

"I stand by that."

Sebastian squirmed out of my hold, started down the stairs, and said, "And it can't be a big bed."

I glanced at our bed in question, then followed him. "It's a comfortable bed, though."

"But the enjoyment of the trope is its forced proximity,"

Sebastian answered. He reached the bottom and turned to watch me coming down the remaining steps. "Having the characters share an intimate space *before* they're ultimately together."

"I didn't realize romance had so many rules."

"It's not all that different from understanding character archetypes in mysteries," he concluded before sitting on the couch.

I joined him as the same animated meteorologist exclaimed that Manhattan was going to get an estimated fifteen to twenty inches of snow by tomorrow morning, with Brooklyn expecting—

The power snapped off suddenly, plunging the apartment into a near-pitch blackness.

"Well, crap," Sebastian stated.

I shifted on the cushion, pushed aside the curtain behind the couch, and took a look through the fogged-up window. "The entire street is out."

Sebastian's phone screen turned on—a sudden beacon in the darkness. He grumbled while dialing down the brightness level, then tapped out what looked like a text message. "I reported the outage to—"

I threw one of the couch pillows at his head.

"Son of a bitch, Calvin!" Sebastian dropped his phone and the screen cast an oddly angled illumination on his face from the floor. He shot me a very unamused expression while fixing his glasses.

"We're going to be stuck here a while." I tugged the blanket from the back of the couch and shook it out.

"What?"

I brought my legs up, stretched out across the couch, then draped the blanket over me. "And it's going to get cold real fast." The sheer puzzlement on Sebastian's face was almost enough to make me laugh and break the pretense. I had to bite the inside of my cheek in order to maintain the scene.

"Our building has a boiler—"

"Don't be an obstinate fool," I snapped.

"*Obstinate fool*?" he slowly repeated. "Are you okay?"

I shifted onto my side, raised the blanket in invitation, and gave his thigh a nudge with my foot. "Stop getting all twisted up about this, Snow. We're conserving body heat, not fucking."

Sebastian's brows knitted together and he opened his mouth to further protest, but then I watched the realization slowly settle into his expression. The hard lines around his eyes and forehead softened, and a lopsided, handsome smile found its way across his face. "Oh."

"So are you getting in the bed or not?"

Sebastian collected his phone and said, "It might not be safe." He leaned toward me and whispered, "There's a danger bigger than the storm."

"Like what?"

"I don't know. The mafia? Bigfoot? It doesn't matter."

"Ah. Okay." I cleared my throat and channeled a bit of the authority I usually reserved for overseeing crime scenes. "The door's barricaded and I'm armed."

Sebastian's smile grew and he nodded minutely in encouragement.

"And… and we'll sleep in shifts. I'll take first watch."

Sebastian looked down at his phone, scratched the tip of his nose absently, then said, with just a hint of attitude, "Fine." He turned the screen off, set the phone aside, and lay with his back to my chest. "But I swear to God, if I so much as feel your dick twitch, Winter, I'm taking it and your balls as spoils of war."

"*Jesus, baby.*" I draped the blanket over Sebastian. Once

we'd settled in and stopped shifting to get comfortable, the apartment became eerily still. The New York City street was silent. It almost did feel as if we were trapped in some isolated manor and not in the heart of the East Village. "What happens now?" I asked, after the moment had stretched on long enough.

"Usually there's a lot of internal drama about being so close, wanting to give in, but not being able to," Sebastian remarked.

"Why can't they?"

"Someone's in a relationship or—you know, something suitably angsty."

"I see." I slipped a hand underneath the blanket and brought it to rest on Sebastian's thigh. I shifted, pressed up harder against him before he could turn, and kissed his exposed neck. "Every minute of every day I've wanted this— wanted you," I whispered against his skin. I brought my hand up, slipped it underneath his T-shirt, and felt Sebastian's stomach flutter against my touch. "I can't breathe when I'm around you, but when you're gone, I feel like I'm dying."

Sebastian's voice hitched as he breathed in.

I splayed my hand against his chest and kissed his neck again. I gave the skin a gentle bite and then a longer suck, because Sebastian was a total pushover for a good hickey, even though he never missed an opportunity to complain about it the next day. "We don't have to ever talk about it," I continued. "When the sun rises tomorrow—when we get out of this place—you'll be Snow and I'll be Winter and nothing had to have happened. I promise."

Sebastian pushed back against me as he tried to roll over. "Calvin," he said, and there was a sort of desperation in his voice that made my heart feel as if it were being squeezed in a vise.

"Yeah, baby?"

Sebastian was partially hanging off the couch after he managed to shift onto his back. He grabbed the back of my head, pulled me down into a kiss, and pressed his tongue against my own. He tasted like hops and cake—a little bitter, a little sweet—and that seemed to wholly encompass who Sebastian was.

"Were we supposed to give in?" I murmured against his mouth.

"No," Sebastian answered, and he started to fall off the edge.

I shot an arm out, pushed the coffee table back, and fell to the floor with him, chasing Sebastian with kisses the entire way down.

C.S. Poe is a Lambda Literary and two-time EPIC award finalist, and a FAPA award-winning author of gay mystery, romance, and speculative fiction.

She resides in New York City, but has also called Key West and Ibaraki, Japan, home in the past. She has an affinity for all things cute and colorful and a major weakness for toys. C.S. is an avid fan of coffee, reading, and cats. She's rescued two cats—Milo and Kasper do their best to distract her from work on a daily basis.

C.S. is an alumna of the School of Visual Arts.

Her debut novel, *The Mystery of Nevermore*, was published 2016.

cspoe.com

ALSO BY C.S. POE

SERIES:
Snow & Winter
The Mystery of Nevermore
The Mystery of the Curiosities
The Mystery of the Moving Image
The Mystery of the Bones

Snow & Winter Collection
Interlude

Magic & Steam
The Engineer
The Gangster

A Lancaster Story
Kneading You
Joy
Color of You

The Silver Screen
Lights. Camera. Murder.

An Auden & O'Callaghan Mystery
(co-written with Gregory Ashe)
A Friend in the Dark
A Friend in the Fire

NOVELS:
Southernmost Murder

NOVELLAS:
11:59

SHORT STORIES:
Love in 24 Frames
That Turtle Story
New Game, Start
Love Has No Expiration

Visit cspoe.com for free slice-of-life codas, titles in audio, and available foreign translations.

Join C.S. Poe's mailing list to stay updated on upcoming releases, sales, conventions, and more!
bit.ly/CSPoeNewsletter